ENCOUNTER AT VILAHANA

FIRST CENTURION KOSNETT, BOOK 1

BLAZE WARD

KNOTTED ROAD PRESS

Encounter at Vilahana
First Centurion Kosnett, Book 1
Blaze Ward
Copyright © 2021 Blaze Ward
All rights reserved
Published by Knotted Road Press
www.KnottedRoadPress.com

ISBN: 978-1-64470-232-1

Cover art:
Illustration 14754337 © Luca Oleastri | Dreamstime.com

Cover and interior design copyright © 2021 Knotted Road Press

Reviews
It's true. Reviews help. Even a short one, such as, "Loved it!" So please consider reviewing this book (and all of the ones you've read) on your favorite retailer site.

Never miss a release!
If you'd like to be notified of new releases, sign up for my newsletter.

http://www.blazeward.com/newsletter/

Buy More!
Did you know that you can buy directly from my website?

https://www.blazeward.com/shop/

This book is licensed for your personal enjoyment only. All rights reserved. This is a work of fiction. All characters and events portrayed in this book are fictional, and any resemblance to real people or incidents is purely coincidental. This book, or parts thereof, may not be reproduced in any form without permission.

The Jessica Keller Chronicles

Auberon

Queen of the Pirates

Last of the Immortals

Goddess of War

Flight of the Blackbird

The Red Admiral

St. Legier

Winterhome

Petron

CS-405

Queen Anne's Revenge

Packmule

Persephone

Additional Alexandria Station Stories

Siren

Two Bottles of Wine with a War God

The Story Road

The Science Officer Series Season One

The Science Officer

The Mind Field

The Gilded Cage

CONTENTS

For 'Alison With One L' and the Ambassador

PROLOGUES

CHAPTER ONE

Phil Kosnett, Explorer Extraordinaire!

For a long moment, he felt like he was back on the bridge of *CS-405*, deep in the old Altai region of *Buran*, before that mad god had finally been slain. Trapped behind enemy lines and deciding to take the war to them instead of surrendering, or just escaping.

However, the moment passed quickly.

Phil had been home for more than seven years now, yet there were still nights he woke in a cold sweat. Tonight, it was probably all the strange bodies all around him.

Given his druthers, he would have done this low-key. A night with close friends and family, since he wasn't likely to be home to celebrate his birthday with everyone for a while.

But First Lord had absolutely put her foot down on this one. And it hadn't been worth yelling at his boss over. Probably.

Phil was having second thoughts as he looked around.

The cake was gone. Cakes. His new Master of the Wardroom had decided to go all in on impressing the new Fleet Centurion who would shortly be in command. Centurion Bottenberg was a hard character to really get to know. They were one hell of a fantastic chef.

Right now, Phil had managed a lull. He'd been exuding *bonhomie* for the last two hours because the party was huge, spanning two decks and at least seventeen rooms, with spillover guaranteed, as many bodies as Petia had apparently invited.

Was anybody actually at work?

Now, he was tired.

He had a glass of red wine in one hand and was using his height and mass maybe a little more offensively than necessary to plow through shorter and smaller bodies. Still it had gotten him to a quiet corner in a room with no chairs. Not many people in here, and most of them looked like bitey introverts, so they'd leave him alone if he didn't try to suck all their energy out.

Phil smiled and nodded amiably. Probably as good as it was going to get.

"There you are," a voice intruded. "Sorry."

The man was much quieter when he stepped into the room, after all the dirty looks and hostile glares he was getting, Fleet Centurion or not.

Phil had found a comfortable spot against a wall, and gestured the man over. They could talk here, if they were quiet. At worst, the folks in here might leave. Nobody was likely to yell at the Guest of Honor, after all.

Fleet Centurion Raizō Tanaka. Commander *RAN Kongō*. One of the new Bedrov-designed Heavy Dreadnoughts, like Keller had taken to war with *Buran* when she commanded *RAN Vanguard*.

An old friend from the Academy, and later from when they were both assigned to the light cruiser *RAN Kamakura*, where Phil had been First Officer right before taking command of *CS-405*. And sailing into the history books. Or something.

"Happy birthday, Phil," Raizō said in a much quieter voice as he got close. "Good luck."

Phil nodded. They touched glasses for a quick toast and drank.

"How's Xui Yi taking all this?" Raizō asked with a twinkle in his eye.

"A bit grumpy," Phil replied with a sad smile. "If Yi Wen and Yong Sheng were a little older, I could have seen her coming along on this mission, but the kids are both in high school and finally settled for the first time in their lives. And on *Ladaux*, so uprooting everyone for this was a little too much. They're all around here somewhere."

"And First Lord wouldn't delay the mission?" Raizō commiserated.

"She stuck me at the Academy for three years to hide me from everyone while she built the ship and the squadron, Raizō," Phil laughed. "Had to have me doing time in grade as a Fleet Centurion so she could work on various Senators to finally give me the fifth stripe."

"Like that was ever in doubt?" his old friend chuckled.

"Lots of people on the shore now," Phil said with a sigh. "Too many officers for too few billets. Be glad they built a new ship in *Kongō* and gave you something to do."

"I had heard a rumor that they considered attaching *Kongō* to your mission," Raizō smiled. "That would have been fun."

"Maybe," Phil countered. "But this is an exploration mission, and everything we've been able to find out third hand suggests that nobody over there is within maybe a century of where the Republic is technologically, after our two hard wars. Three if you measure how close we came to a civil war over the *Horvat Incident*. Showing up with a Heavy Dreadnought sends the wrong message."

"And a Survey Dreadnought doesn't?" Raizō pressed.

"When you take out the Bubble Gun and two of the Type-4s, the ship is a lot less intimidating, and it opens up a huge amount of space, so we could haul a massively oversized Ambassadorial force, as well as install a complete arboretum to trade plants and seeds with whoever we meet out there."

Raizō fell silent for a moment. Phil did likewise. His old

partner in crime from the Academy days had an evil look in his eyes.

"Who would have imagined where we're end up," Raizō said. "What ever happened to that one girl you were dating, back in school?"

"Unhelpful," Phil glared at the man. "Which one?"

"The planetary development expert, you know, the blonde from New Georgia? What was her name?" Raizō asked.

"Alison," Phil replied. "Alison Smith. *Doctor* Alison Smith, last I heard, but that was maybe fifteen years ago."

"Not the marrying type?" Raizō pressed, studying him.

"Maybe, in another life," Phil said with a shrug. "If I'd ended up in academia, or maybe gone into government service as a bureaucrat or diplomat instead of being a sailor. She had never struck me as the type that would happily remain at home alone while I was off flying starships. Too vibrant. Too smart. Too alive."

Phil shrugged. Add that to the other things that occasionally haunted him. Far less fearsome than a broken JumpSail in enemy territory. Probably. Alison had been one hell of a woman.

"There you are," another voice intruded.

This time, the restless stirring turned into bodies suddenly in motion towards the door.

Phil figured that a Senior Centurion would likely be getting yelled at by a Master Chief, if the ranks in this room were different. But he was a First Centurion, Raizō a Fleet Centurion, and the First Lord of the Fleet had just walked in.

Or rather, gotten stuck in the hallway as bodies rushed the door to escape *all the damned noise.*

Petia Naoumov. She was tall for a woman, almost as tall as Phil. The long, black hair that had been her signature for so long was coming in mostly gray now, but Phil didn't know if that was the stress of the job or maybe she'd always dyed it before finally deciding she didn't have to anymore.

They were close, but there were some questions you didn't ask any woman you weren't married to.

"No, don't go anywhere Tanaka," Pet said as they suddenly had the small room to themselves.

Phil suppressed yet another sigh and considered his boss.

His current boss. It was no secret that she would retire soon, having mostly held on this long so she could send Phil into the darkness on this last great mission. Arott Whughy would take over as First Lord after Phil left, unless something revolutionary happened in the Republic Senate.

Again.

"Time for official pictures, Phil," Pet said with a smile. "I need something for my brag wall."

Phil laughed out loud. Nils Kasum had won the war with the *Fribourg Empire*, but Pet had topped it and beaten *Buran*. As well as held the Navy and the Republic together when Horvat nearly broke both. All Phil had done was face down an Imperial fleet big enough to grind his little squadron into paste, deal with the future Imperial Consort, Vo *zu* Arlo, and supply the paperwork that brought down his own entire government and eventually watched several death sentences be commuted to life imprisonment for formerly-important Senators.

"Why me?" Raizō asked with a hint of a teenager asked to clean his room. But he'd been another of Pet's projects over the years.

"Everyone Command Centurion and above," Pet ordered. "Plus everyone who ever served with Phil, whatever ship or command. We're making history here, so we should record and remember it. This group will never assemble again. Besides, I'm the boss and I get to order you mere Centurions around."

She was grinning. Phil was grinning. Hell, even normally-quiet Raizō was grinning.

But all beginnings require endings. This might truly be the end of two centuries of near-constant warfare for the Republic, that they could send a Survey Dreadnought, a Survey Cruiser, and a support squadron deep across the belt of darkness marked *Galactic West* on standard nav charts.

Once you got beyond the galactic arm then stars became thin. Spread out. Neither *Aquitaine* nor anyone else had really expanded that way, when there were so many stars the other directions.

Now, with peace everywhere, it was time to finally look out there and see what there was to behold.

And he got to be the one to go.

Phil Kosnett, Explorer Extraordinaire!

CHAPTER TWO

Phil looked around the space that would be his new office for the next few years, if he was lucky. Three years of teaching at the Academy and he had always been surrounded by books, so he was excited that he had more space here and less need to stop and look something obscure up when grading papers or preparing a lecture.

Now, he had an actual office, **AND** he was on a starship again, after an occasionally star-crossed career unlike anything he'd ever imagined since the day he first got his acceptance letter to the Academy. His last command, at least he presumed, but Phil wasn't worried or upset with that. The Academy would take him back in a heartbeat as a civilian. Or he could maybe try to get promoted to one of the civilian Lords of the Fleet when he got home.

Whughy would be in charge by then. Phil figured he had an outside chance of succeeding Arott when that man was done, though it would depend on a lot of things not in Phil's control.

And he had to want it.

Phil still wasn't sure he did. At this point, it didn't matter, as that was years in the future.

Right now, he had paperwork to do.

Or did. A knock at the door interrupted him. A moment later, Markus opened it and peeked in.

"Special courier just delivered a package for you, sir," he said.

Senior Chief Markus Dunklin. Former engineer on *CS-405*. Still a crazy redneck armorer. Phil had gone and found that boy for this mission, one of the few he'd called in favors to get.

"Show me your hands," Phil ordered.

Markus entered and put a package on the desk, then held up both hands, palms in.

For all that crazy boy liked to weld and play with things that went boom, he had not damaged his fingers.

"All ten, First Centurion," Markus smiled.

"You know the rules, Dunklin," Phil laughed as the rascal fled.

As long as the man still had all ten, he could be Phil's personal assistant. His *dog robber*, like Marcelle Travere had done for Jessica for so long.

Phil figured he needed a crazy redneck with an understanding of making and using primitive firearms, where he was going. Markus had been one of the plankholders when they first captured the *Buran* freighter that Siobhan had ended up naming *Queen Anne's Revenge*.

Back when they were all pirates.

Phil studied the package in front of him after the door closed. Maybe thirty centimeters wide. Forty long. Fifteen deep. Simple cardstock container with a slip-on lid.

Phil pulled the lid off and saw two presents wrapped inside, one big and flat, one narrow and long.

He wondered who had missed his birthday last week in shipping something some great distance. Jessica hadn't been here, but had sent messages to be delivered by as many veterans of *The Expedition* as were there to see him off. Most of the big names were retired these days and many had been here physically.

Someone had written 'Open me first' on the flat one, so Phil set aside the one that was shaped like a bottle of wine in a box. It was too light, so he had no clue what it contained.

When opened up, the flat one turned out to be a leather-bound journal with an ink pen in the ancient style, along with a letter tucked in that he opened next.

First Centurion Kosnett,

We cannot be there to see you off, nor to assist in the grand undertaking, but I hope that you might be induced to write some notes and observations in the journal as you go, in the manner of the ancient ship captains of Earth, sailing distant oceans. To record those things that might not make your official logs for being too poetical, too romantic, too something *for the mere warriors and bureaucrats back home to appreciate.*

I am also sending along a recording of a new symphony I wrote, inspired by those ancient voyages, as well as my dreams of what you might find when you seek a new horizon, with audio by the Royal Symphony of Werder. May it bring you peace and inspiration.

Casey Weigand, Centurion, RAN, retired.

Phil opened the notebook and found the chip containing the music, as well as the pen, tucked into a little strap. He laughed to himself, wondering how well that young woman had really known him, even though they had never spent much time in direct communication.

He was especially charmed that Karl VIII, *Emperor of Fribourg By Grace of God and hereditary King of St. Legier* had left off **all** her other titles, including the *zu* to which she had earned even before ascending, as though being a Centurion in the *Republic of Aquitaine* Navy was the single highest honor one might hold. Still, at one time she had wanted nothing more from life, and but for *Buran*, might have achieved it and be sitting up on his bridge right now, about to command Phil's own flagship in this voyage.

Phil could only imagine what that future would have looked like. Still, everyone makes choices that turn corners irrevocably.

He moved on to the other box and opened it, finding a letter resting atop.

> *Kosnett,*
>
> *As First Lord Kasum has said, it was our job to stand atop the wall facing the darkness, and by doing so, defy it. At Hemera, you took that charge to heart and stood steady, at a time when I might have annihilated you.*
>
> *I hope that this present will help you see yet farther than you already do, which is beyond what most people imagine, let alone achieve. I am only sorry that I could not go with you.*
>
> *Arlo*

Imperial General and Aquitaine Centurion Vo *zu* Arlo, *Imperial Consort* and *Ritter of the Imperial Household.* And a dozen other titles and legends, all of which rated the man an absolute hero on a scale with Jessica Keller herself. And the commander who had been across the line that day at *Hemera*, even when they were both *RAN* to the soul.

Arlo understood.

Phil pulled the object out and realized that it was a brass telescope in the most ancient style, with four sections that would expand, one inside the other, and lens at both ends. Useless at the sorts of distances a starship did things, but like Casey, a hearkening back to the older eras, when civilians and sailors went to sea and then to space, looking beyond that next horizon.

He pulled out a small cloth bag designed presumably to keep the brass safe from salty air then looked for a spot on a nearby shelf. He had a single bookcase in here, unlike his academy office, that was already about half full with things he wanted to be able to sit and read in the evening, including a copy of Wachturm's *Jessica Keller, Volume One*, as well as Voisson's *The Modern History of the Republic*.

Both were out of date, as neither even considered the galaxy that the last ten years had become. They were here because they spoke to him of things that had been. There were rumors that Wachturm was writing *Volume Two*, so maybe Phil had that to look forward to when he got back.

The telescope was at eye level when he was standing, stationed upright. If it was real brass, presumably Dunklin would need to find a way to keep it clean. Phil just knew that the redneck would look on it as a challenge, so Phil wasn't concerned. The notebook stayed on his desk for now.

This was his duty office, just off the flag bridge of *RAN Urumchi*. His personal cabin also had a small office. Keller had always slept in a regular officer's cabin, when she was aboard *RAN Vanguard*, but that was Keller, and she was a warrior first and foremost.

Urumchi didn't have the bubble gun, so that opened a lot of space down the ship's centerline. Part of it was filled with the arboretum. At the same time, Phil had chosen to take an Ambassadorial suite for himself, mostly because he figured he would be entertaining guests, just about anywhere he went. Thus, it would be nice to be able to do something small and cozy, like a dinner party with a dozen folks, rather than the huge events you got at planetary receptions.

And it kept him close to all the various accredited Ambassadors he was hauling. Couldn't have just one, when you didn't know how many worlds you might visit, so he had a plethora and a half. Or maybe three quarters. The semantics of it always eluded him.

Phil checked the time and decided he was close enough. He slipped the journal under his arm and opened the outer hatch. Dunklin had never been a spit-and-polish sailor, except when handling explosives, so he did not immediately jump to his feet. Phil appreciated that about the man.

"Who's next?" Markus asked.

"You stay here and guard the fort," Phil said with a smile. "Gonna go pull a surprise inspection on the bridge."

Markus laughed and went back to whatever he had been reading on his tablet.

Phil looked around the flag bridge, but everyone was generally paying attention to screens, and he had a standing order that nobody was to announce him in here. His ego did not require people stopping what they were doing just to stand up, nod at him, and sit back down.

And today, he had something special in mind and wanted to sneak up on her.

CHAPTER THREE

Heather Lau still found it weird, being aboard the bridge of a Bedrov-designed ship again. She'd spent the last four years in command of *RAN Jellicoe*, an *Admiral*-class Heavy Cruiser of the old style. Before *CS-405* or her first proper command, *CE-419*. *RAN Packmule* didn't really count, legends and lies notwithstanding.

But a lot of the oldest boats were being decommissioned these days, replaced by maybe one new hull for three old ones going away. *Jellicoe* had been one of them, and Heather had figured at the time that she didn't have the seniority for her own expeditionary cruiser.

And then Phil had called.

She looked up from her screen as the bridge suddenly got deathly silent around her. She saw that ghost, grinning at her from just inside the hatch. But the First Centurion was like that. Professorial, without being pedantic about things like standing up when he entered the room.

"Yes, sir?" she asked laconically.

Nobody had come to attention, so she didn't even bother unbuckling. Besides, Bedrov had understood how to design comfortable command chairs.

"I wanted to drag *Ground Control* off for a quick update," Phil said with a grin.

Ground Control. Her pirate nickname that only a very few people were ever allowed to use in public. Five, out of this entire crew, as a matter of fact, but they'd all been there with her.

"Just me?" she asked, one eyebrow rising.

Phil looked around the room, noting faces. He'd only come aboard longer than a day or a weekend since July, while she'd spent six months working up this crew before that and organizing all the support vessels that would travel with them. However, that was part of the reason Phil had wanted her.

Like him, she'd been on the far side of the darkness and had to make do with whatever you could make, steal, or repurpose. They were about to be a long ways from home on this one. Not as far as *Ninagirsu*, to say nothing of *Winterhome*, but there were precious few inhabited stars going west.

"Just you," Phil decided after a moment.

"Iveta, you have the flag," Heather said, turning to her First Officer and noting the gleam of joy and lust that frequently came into the woman's eyes at those words.

Senior Centurion Iveta Beridze was another one in the Jessica Keller mold. The Navy had a bunch of them in their mid-thirties, fired up by Keller's exploits in the Great War and honed by *The Expedition.*

Forever planning. Forever studying. Forever thinking.

There wasn't likely to be much in the way of martial glory on a survey mission like this, but that didn't stop Beridze from being prepared. Or any of the rest of them. Being under the command of a former pirate like Heather didn't help, as many of them had starting studying her old adventures almost as closely as they did Keller's.

Weird.

Heather followed Phil back out into the corridor and turned forward, walking beside the man. These hallways were wider than *Jellicoe's*, so she kept subconsciously thinking she was on a station somewhere, instead of a dreadnought.

"Where are we headed?" she asked.

Not for anything in particular, so much as to pass the time.

"Go see Sergey," Phil replied with a grin.

Heather laughed.

Bubble Gun systems were huge installations. Not much smaller than the corvette she'd commanded after she'd stopped being Phil's First Officer. Taking that out gave them space for a forest, which had in turn required a master gardener, who was a civilian. And who was damned sure going to remind you of that any time you forgot.

Neither the bridge where she sat nor flag bridge were all that far away from it, seated right behind the space, almost at the center of the vessel.

They passed through the airlock into the place Heather always thought of as the Garden of Eden. Dirt. Bushes. Trees. A path that looked like it was stones resting on the ground, but were actually the tops of columns more than two meters deep, with soil packed in and meshed in various places to hold it while the roots grew every which way.

They were alone. But only for a moment, as Sergey Cummins appeared from whatever he'd been doing inside the depth of greenery around them.

"Oh, it's you," he said, nodding then promptly ignoring them and returning to the heavy brush.

Heather grinned at the man's back. He was a civilian master gardener, who didn't care a fig for the military way of doing things.

"And stay out of my blueberries," Sergey's voice carried back a moment later. "They are ripe and I'm going to make syrup from them."

"Yes, Sergey," Heather called. "Thank you."

Phil grinned and led her deeper into the jungle. They were

alone save for whatever insects and small birds might be flitting about.

"So what's really on your mind, Phil?" Heather asked.

Phil stopped walking and turned to look at her. She was tall, but he was taller. Four years senior to her, though Heather didn't figure she'd ever earn her fourth stripe. *RAN Urumchi* and this mission might be a great way to retire.

"Thinking about *Lighthouse Station*," Phil said.

Heather flashed back to a cattle and chicken ranch they had built up in the middle of *Buran*, back during the war. Stealing cattle and chickens from another world. And horses for the Duke as well as *CS-405*'s former Boatswain, Bok Battenhouse.

"Think we'll need to do something similar out there?" Heather asked, midway between serious and chuckling.

"Hoping that we'll find some of those civilized folks and nations that are really just legends and tall tales, this far away on the galactic disk," he replied. "But at the same time, having *Lighthouse* meant that we were set without having to return home. And it gave *zu* Wachturm and Kasum a forward base when they set out to pacify and trade, after we killed a god."

"We're not entirely prepared to build such a thing, if you happen to find an empty world, Phil," Heather said, still smiling. "Should I stop and requisition some retired cowboys from Fourth Saxon Legion to go with us? Maybe find an escort carrier configured for horses and cattle?"

"I'd say very funny right now, but that's at the back of my mind," Phil said. "We're taking a pair of bastions or a full citadel, just so we have a secured point that should be proof against anything but fleets. And the new *Baja*-class Fast Clippers will still be running a long haul each way to bring us fresh socks if I decide I need cowboys."

"So what planning should I do?" Heather pressed.

"Maybe turn Iveta loose on it." It was Phil's turn to laugh. "Give her something weird to do. Just don't let her seduce Markus too much."

"Dunklin?" Heather blinked in surprise.

"Dunno if I'm imagining it, but those two seem to have chemistry," Phil said. "And he's not in her chain of command, so that would help. Plus, he was there at *Lighthouse*, so he would be the best person for her to interview."

"Huh."

Heather made a note to inquire with some of her more efficient gossips. It was useful, having people willing to share tidbits with the boss, without necessarily attributing names to things.

"What else?" she asked.

"That's it," Phil sighed. "I've spent nearly four years thinking about this. You've spent most of this year working on people, once I got you the key players. But we're kind of back to *Severnaya Zemlya* and everything that happened afterwards. I'm going to point us in a direction, and hopefully be busy dealing with governments and all my ambassadorial ducks here, while you're going to be on your own for mundane things. That's exactly why I needed you, and not any of the others who applied for this slot, Heather. First Centurions, Jessica excepted as in all things, are not supposed to turn over squadron operations to the Command Centurion and ignore it. Denis Jež could handle it. You can, too."

"*Ground Control*," Heather replied.

"If we're that far out, I want someone thinking like a pirate," Phil smiled. "Besides, I can't imagine that anywhere we go isn't already going to have some sort of piracy or smuggling issue. Nature of the beast. We just need to figure out how to talk to those people, too."

Heather laughed and they turned to head back into the mechanical part of the ship.

Phil was going to be the diplomat.

She was doing piracy again.

CHAPTER FOUR

Phil studied the flag bridge around him, aware that everyone was on pins and needles. It was time.

He was seated in the command chair, like Jessica always had been, back on the Star Controller *Auberon* and later on the Heavy Dreadnought *Vanguard*. Directly across the table from him was Command Centurion Harinder Abbatelli, his flag centurion.

As with most of this mission, things were heavily tilted to more senior ranks than it might have been a decade ago. Partly, that was the end of the various wars and the general demobilization of the five major players in this part of space. Lots of officers stranded on the beach, or facing it and available for slots on new exploration missions.

However, Phil had also known he needed older heads on this mission. This wasn't conquest, or even warfare. He was going out and tracing down other places so far away that they didn't trade with *Aquitaine* or anyone else over here, the galactic distances being so great.

So he had a Command Centurion across from him. Harinder was one of Enej Zivkovic's former students, and brilliant at what she did, which was the paperwork side of things.

Physically, the woman was almost the exact opposite of Heather Lau, being short and curvy, with darker skin than almost anyone Phil knew who wasn't African Diaspora. Eyes nearly black, but gleaming like cut stones as she watched him.

"Bring everybody into the circuit," Phil ordered, starting the ball rolling.

Or the avalanche tumbling, depending on how you wanted to look at it.

On the screen in front of him, sixteen faces appeared, fourteen Command Centurions from the various ships and the Fleet Diplomat in charge of all the ambassadors *Urumchi* was hauling, plus Fleet Machinist Valeriev, the woman who would be in command of the castle that Phil was hauling with him.

Arott Whughy had done something similar for *The Expedition*, and turned into First Lord of the Fleet, so Phil had had his pick there, as well.

Everyone here had been approved by Phil, after some long nights spent with Pet and her staff, going over files. People who came highly rated from his friends, former crew, and commanders, even if Phil only knew a few of them.

Pet had specifically built him this fleet, like Kasum had built *First Expeditionary* for Jessica.

They would hold.

"*RAN Urumchi*," Phil began, seemingly at random, feeling like being *The Professor* for a bit. "Named for the town on the northwest corner of what had been the Great Wall of China, back when Earth was a place Humans could live. The place where the fabled Silk Road itself began, before heading into the desert and eventually connecting to the Islamic world of Central Asia and the Christian one of Europe."

Heather nodded on the screen.

"*RAN Viking*, named for an early Human exploration program, as far back as the Industrial Age on Earth," he continued. "To that, we add *CT-9503* hauling our forward operating base. Command Corvette *CC-501*, Battle Corvette *CB-502*, and the Guardians: *CG-503*, *CG-504*, *CG-505*, *CG-506*, as well as the minesweeper *CM-507*. *Baja*-class Fast Clippers *Mexicali*, *Ensenada*, *Tecate*, and *San Quintin*."

Each of his commanders nodded or reacted. This might be the last big adventure of their careers, and all had fought hard to be here when the First Lord had announced this building program.

The last great adventure?

Phil doubted it. That was why he'd brought Heather and Markus. Why he had a specifically-non-Republic citizen as his Chief Medical Officer. They were going alien places, and Sam Au didn't think like the rest of these crews. And she'd been with him at *Lighthouse Station*, as had her husband, the notorious pirate *Stunt Dude*, who had retired to seek her out and refused to come back into uniform as *Urumchi*'s Dragoon.

Next big adventure. That was better.

"We didn't take a dreadnought like *Kongō* on this mission because we're about trade and diplomacy," Phil continued, drawing everyone into a lecture now, rather than firing them up to storm the gates of hell like Keller had always had a knack for. "It would have sent the wrong message to the people we met, to bring warships."

He paused and drew a breath, again noting that weird mix of relaxed tension on all these faces.

"Make no mistake though, we can protect ourselves," Phil reminded everyone. "*Urumchi* might be a survey dreadnought, but she's still got a pair of Type-4s. *Viking* might be a survey cruiser, but she's almost as well armed as we are. The corvettes are all *Scorpion*-class variants, after that pirate and I had a long talk about things he did wrong with the *Expeditionary*-class, like *CS-405*. He listened. First Centurion Whughy gave us the Pulse-Two. The Fast Clippers are bigger and faster than the California-class Fleet Replenishment Freighters that had been the backbone of the support fleet for so long. We are ready."

Every face blinked in perfect unison. It helped that Phil had just spent three years teaching both Command Ethics and Advanced Piracy at the Academy. He knew how to hold his students, draw them in like a trapdoor spider, and then educate them when they weren't looking.

"So we are about to make history, my friends," Phil smiled at the various faces. "*CM-507*, you have the van. Break orbit now and begin your acceleration. All vessels conform to *CM-507* in lines astern and prepare to jump. Heather, you have the flag."

THE BALHEE CLUSTER

CHAPTER FIVE

"All hands, stand by for combat," Commander Kaur Singh announced to the vessel over the main system, hearing her voice come out of the speakers behind her, just as it would in every room aboard the heavy cruiser *Aranyani*.

The *Aditi Consensus* didn't frequently inject itself into worlds like *Vilahana*, but that was because they just tried to keep the peace. It was not worth the effort that attempting to conquer and hold other worlds in the face of the resistance such a move would generate.

Most of the time.

"Helm, how long until we exit JumpSpace?" she asked.

Her raised command chair had a good view of the bridge crew. Forward on her left, with his back to her, Officer Misra was piloting the massive warship towards their rendezvous with one of those worlds that probably qualified as a pirate outpost, although any paperwork they produced would be close enough to legitimate to pass.

The star nation known as the *Aditi Consensus* did not reach this far. Singh had to rely on this ship, *Aranyani*, as her war chariot, and this crew as her army. This whole mission left a sour taste in her mouth.

Which was why Senior Officer Nagarkar was on Misra's right, charging the Power Tap and loading all four titan bolts, in case battle was the answer the pirates gave her when she demanded that the pirates return the ship and ambassador they had captured.

Kaur Singh only really cared about one freighter when they got there, and then only because it had been quietly hauling an ambassador to *Troeg* when a pirate warship suddenly appeared and captured it.

She was here to take it back.

"One minute, Commander," Misra replied without looking back over his shoulder.

"Nagarkar, prime the capacitors for all the Main and Point Guns," she ordered next.

"Already complete, Commander." Namrata Nagarkar did glance back, but it was just to smile, as she had gone ahead and preempted her commander with such a move.

But they all knew what was coming.

"Center the Shield Projector forward," Kaur ordered.

It could spin any direction, but she would probably have them all in front of her when she emerged. That extra layer of defense would give the pirates pause.

An *Aditi* heavy cruiser was a fearsome beast, especially as most pirate vessels tended to be second-hand frigates and destroyers, frequently of *Dalou* construction, since the *Hegemony* would export to anyone with the cash.

If the pirates were feeling feisty, they might have sufficient numbers to swarm her, but Kaur expected them to merely run like flushed quail.

"Exiting JumpSpace now," Misra called loudly, reminding everyone that they were now in enemy territory, if the governor of *Vilahana* chose to interpret it that way.

"Sensors?" Kaur called.

"Stand by," Sub-Commander Arya Chaudhari replied, face

down on her special three-dimensional projector. "Projecting the forward array now."

Commander Singh watched the display at the front of the round room change from mere stars in the distance to a two-dimensional plot, showing a slice of the planet and several orbital stations, plus the requisite minefields amidst the junkyards with their claim beacons and one-person tugs hauling things back like sheep dogs after strays.

"Freighter *RBQWH-486148* confirmed in high orbit," Chaudhari said as one of the dots above the planet turned bright red.

There were a lot of other ships visible. More than usual.

"Add a filter to eliminate anything smaller than a warship," Kaur ordered. "Also remove big freighters. I want to see just the folks with guns."

Hard to do, she appreciated, as any vessel could have a few gun turrets welded on later, especially in a pirate haven, but unless they had been built to military standards, they were not a threat to *Aranyani*. Even a few dozen of them all at once.

She only regretted not having been in a position to have brought a couple of smaller warships with her. Forming a Phalanx right now with a couple of porcupines or wolverines in front of her would have shut every pirate commander down right now, or sent them running as fast they could exit the gravity well and flee her.

Kaur Singh was here to rescue one ship, and the ambassador.

The screen blinked once and only seven ships were visible now. One local battle-tug, broadcasting *Vilahana* colors and serving as something of a semi-mobile battlestation for the system. It would be a threat to *Aranyani*, if they chose. Hell, it would be a threat to a full Ship of the Line, to say nothing of a Stronghold-scale ship like *Aranyani*.

But she wasn't here to fight.

There was a warship parked close to the freighter that had drawn

Aranyani this far from home. The hull looked like it had come from a *Dalou Hegemony* yard, at least originally. Those folks had a messy, nearly feudalistic culture left over from the return to space flight over the last eight hundred years, so *Dalou* privateers were almost as common as the *Zen-Mekyo Syndicates* that preyed on shipping.

When everyone had letters of marque and reprisal from somewhere, separating true pirates from privateers, freedom fighters, and displaced nobles trying to get their inheritance back became a chore.

Easier to achieve Consensus and live as one harmonious whole, but some people were just born mean. Sociopaths incapable of feeling empathy for a total stranger.

Thus the *Aditi Consensus* built the lines of the Phalanx and tried to keep the peace.

"Identify the freighter's consort," Kaur ordered.

"Vessel identifies as *Saluki*," Chaudhari answered quickly. "Word origin: Ancient Egypt. Term for a type of hunting canine. Markings appear identical to the vessel that captured the ambassador."

"Open a hail," Kaur said grimly. "Wide transmission. Might as well let everyone know what we're up to."

"Hailing open, Commander," Chaudhari answered.

"Warship *Saluki*, this is the *Aditi Consensus* cruiser *Aranyani*," Kaur intoned slowly, just in case her sudden exit at the top of the gravity well had somehow gone unnoticed. "Freighter *RBQWH-486148* was transporting an ambassador when it was taken. We have come to retrieve her and the vessel. If you wish to challenge, you may file a complaint in the appropriate Chandlery court, otherwise, you will surrender for boarding immediately."

She turned to look over her right shoulder and signaled her Sub-Commander to cut the transmitter.

"Nagarkar, lock weapons on *Saluki* and make sure they see you do it," she ordered next.

Targeting scanners were loud, if you were listening, a bright spotlight in the face until you raised a shade for your eyes.

"We have redshift on *Saluki*," the Sub-Commander said now. "*Freighter RBQWH-486148* is also powering up engines but they were cold. I estimate that it will take them roughly ten minutes to begin significant maneuvering. *Saluki* is broadcasting ECM at moderate levels."

ECM. Electronic Counter-Measures. Crap on sensor channels designed to obscure and confuse.

About what she expected from a pirate caught with her hand in the cookie jar when Mom arrived.

"Good enough," Kaur said loudly. "Helm, plot and execute a pursuit and intercept course, but make sure not to get too close to any other warships and stay well clear of the battle tug. Nagarkar, stand by for the titan bolts. We'll hold the Power Tap until we get closer."

"Warning shot, sir?" Nagarkar asked.

"Negative," Kaur replied coldly. "They had their warning. They had the ability to politely surrender the ambassador and the ship without weapons. They chose to ignore both and think they can get away from us now. Accelerate on them and make sure they understands that they made a poor choice."

"Understood, sir."

Aranyani had speed and high ground on *Saluki*. The pirate was looking to cut across the orbit of *Vilahana*, but the only way that was happening was if she let him go.

Kaur studied the range. A bit extreme, but closing.

"Use long-range targeting, Nagarkar," Kaur said now. "I'd rather get the hits at a lower damage level."

"Shifting to long-range," Nagarkar replied, rapidly pushing buttons to change the final charging sequence on the titan bolts.

The titan bolt was a warhead with a tremendous capacitor built in. You could set it for long-range, standard, or short-range, depending on your needs, with three different levels of damage if you hit. Long-range would detonate as soon as it got close to the target, which usually meant less damage, but also still hit them for something if the bolt itself might have otherwise missed.

The range was a bit long for standard settings, and she wanted their attention now.

"Fire a spread," Kaur ordered. "All four tubes and begin reloading."

On the screen, four bright dots appeared, racing madly towards the pirate and impacting in less than three seconds. Three hits. Pretty good shooting.

"Their Shield Projector took most of it," Nagarkar called over her shoulder.

"Let them have the Main Guns at extreme range next," Kaur smiled.

Extreme. But Nagarkar was an artist with those beams, and had the feel now. *Dalou* warships were always build with a passive sort of stealth to them in the way the hull was sloped. Made it hard to get a solid ranging ping. Doubly so when the pirate was broadcasting noise.

Four Main Guns fired next, beams lashing out. Two hits, one of which seemed to penetrate the Shield Projector to splash right above the hull itself.

"Shield Projector overloaded, Commander," Nagarkar called with a hard laugh in her tone.

"Let them have the Power Tap now, Namrata," Kaur replied with what she suspected was an equal grin on her face.

The first wave hit as the Power Tap locked onto the target. Like the second Main Gun, the navigation shields held, but Kaur wasn't concerned. She'd caught them before they could start maneuvering enough to slip the leash of the Power Tap's lock.

"Contact on one," Nagarkar announced. "Shields holding."

Kaur smiled and waited. *Aranyani* was racing down on them with every second as they tried to climb out of the gravity well.

Saluki hadn't tried firing anything back at her, but Kaur

wasn't surprised. *Dalou*-style warships were intended to confront a target, with their largest heavy weapon mount centerline forward, like the space dragons they were intended to visually emulate.

If it was a true pirate, or one of *Zen-Mekyo Syndicate* vessels, they might have swapped out the firebird mount for anything, but it was facing the wrong way to engage her, and the Commander over there apparently didn't have as good a Weapons Officer as Namrata Nagarkar.

Not many people did.

"Change screen to animation mode," Kaur called now.

The main screen dropped the area scan, but Kaur knew that Arya would continue watching from her station. Instead, they had a view of *Saluki* as if from much closer, with shields visible as a faint, golden haze around the ship and the pipeline of destruction representing the Power Tap locked on like a leech. Maybe rattlesnake was a more appropriate term, as it was pumping destruction like poison, instead of sucking out blood.

"Second Tap maintains lock," Nagarkar said.

Indeed, on the screen, a second bolt of destruction hit *Saluki*'s shields now and Kaur watched them collapse under the load.

"Commander, I have *Saluki* on the line again, asking for terms," Arya called from her corner of the bridge.

Kaur considered it for a half heartbeat.

"Let them have the third wave directly into his hull and then break the lock, Nagarkar," Kaur ordered. "Shunt the remaining energy for the last wave back into the batteries and start the charging cycle again. Make sure to use long-range targeting on the next spread of titan bolts."

"Understood," Nagarkar said, typing quickly.

Kaur watched intently as the final attack seemed to catch *Saluki* right at the boom line. Like everyone else, *Dalou* ships had a forward boom that could be separated from the rear section, in order to land on a planetary surface, or to escape if the JumpSails, engines, or generators in the aft hull were at risk of detonating.

The little dragon in front of her had two engine nacelles separated from the central hull with double pylons. Probably main gun mounts at the forward end of each, with a big weapon at the "mouth" of the dragon. The head and spine would separate like it was lifting from the ground.

Only the *Dalou* did it that way. Everyone else generally either had two clean sections, forward and aft that just disconnected, or the front would slide backwards into a socket like a sword. The *Ewin Principality* had a weird approach to ship building. Almost as weird as *Yaumgan*.

"*Saluki* has struck their colors," Arya said now.

"Launch a shuttle with a combat team aboard to take possession," Kaur ordered. "Tell the Officer in charge that if the pirates give them any grief to threaten to send a prize crew next. We won't, unless they have more bile than I expect, but I want that ship shut down until I find the ambassador and his staff."

"And if something has happened to him?" Arya asked.

"Then we might organize a trial for piracy," Kaur replied.

Around her, several people blanched or gulped. Senior officer would have to sit on such a board, and the expectation would be executions by hanging afterwards.

Hopefully, the commander on *Saluki* was brighter than that.

CHAPTER SIX

ADCON CRUISER ARANYANI

Kaur was settled on her favorite chair to read. Most of her personal cabin was spartan in furnishing and decoration, but she had taken the effort to replace the chair that the former commander had left her and swap it out for one personally made to her size and shape by an artist with wood and fabric.

Saluki had indeed rolled over and put its feet in the air when they realized that *Aranyani* was serious about destroying them.

Kaur wasn't here to conquer. And she lacked the necessary force to actually do anything about *Vilahana* as a planetary culture, but she could still put the fear of the gods into any pirates out there. Didn't matter if they were *Dalou* privateers, *Gloran* raiders, *Zen-Mekyo* syndicalists, or anybody else.

What you did to each other was your own problem. When you decided to bother the *Aditi Consensus*, you got to deal with people like Kaur Singh.

The door signal chirped and Kaur sighed, putting down her bookreader and keying the door open. She was in the front room of her suite, where she entertained guests, but that didn't mean she was always on duty, regardless of being commander of this ship.

Still, the galaxy never waits.

Arya Chaudhari entered and stood more or less at attention as the hatch closed behind her.

"That bad?" Kaur asked. "Or are you allowed to sit?"

Ayra did grin at that, because she had a reputation as a scholar and something of a stick-in-the-ass believer in rules. Kaur was tall and broad in the shoulders and hips. Arya was just a few centimeters shorter and waify thin, maybe weighing ten kilograms less than Kaur's seventy.

Both women had the black, straight hair that was so common in the *Aditi Consensus*, and the dark eyes and ink-colored skin. Kaur might have been a little darker in both, but not much. And these days her hair was coming in gray underneath, to the point that she had considered cutting it down from medium length with beard trimmers, just to have it all go at once.

A decade younger, Arya only had a few stripes of white so far. She also kept her hair much shorter most of the time.

Arya took the couch and even sat back in it far enough to touch her shoulder blades.

"So the governor of *Vilahana* sent a formal complaint about our actions in his orbital space," Arya began diligently.

Kaur nodded. Nothing unexpected. This was not the first time she'd had to do something like this, though it was the first time she had taken *Aranyani* this far from home to do it.

"And?" she prompted.

"The man followed it up with an invitation for you to call upon him at his palace on the ground," Arya continued.

"Yeah, that's not happening," Kaur replied instantly with a harsh laugh.

Both women shared a smile.

"Invite him up for a state dinner aboard *Aranyani*," Kaur countered. "The worst that can happen is that he takes us up on it."

"How mean are you feeling?" Arya asked, suddenly looking a good deal less prim and proper.

"How evil are *you* feeling?" Kaur salvoed things back at her Sub-Commander.

"As you know, Commander, we have rescued our ambassador," Arya said. "Captured the pirates who did it, all of whom claim the usual legal protections from their homeworlds and such. Additionally, there are a dozen other ships in close orbit, representing gods-only-know how many pirate clans, syndicates, or rogue *Dalou* prefectures. Do we invite all the commanders to dinner?"

Kaur laughed before she could control herself.

"That'd be like throwing chickens to a pack of wolves," she finally grinned.

Arya matched her mirth.

"What's the worst they could do?" she asked, mimicking her boss. "Accept?"

"Do it," Kaur said, sobering and starting to contemplate the political and diplomatic ramifications.

The Balhee Cluster wasn't completely isolated from the rest of the galaxy. At the same time, it represented a kind of island culture well away from the either of the nearest galactic arms. The various birthing nebulae wrapped around them meant that there were really only a few channels in and out, as though the cluster was an enormous lagoon nearly surrounded by impenetrable reefs.

Vilahana happened to sit just about in the middle of one of the largest egresses back into the rest of the galaxy, weirdly pointed almost straight up, relative to the galactic plane. Merchants called here, coming and going on missions to some of those impossible distances to the arms. At the same time, news traveled slowly.

Kaur might learn useful things from the governor or other commanders, if she had them all in a room and having to behave, under threat of her combat teams if anyone decided to challenge someone to a duel. The *Aditi Consensus* was almost at the center of the hollow sphere, surrounded on all sides by others. The largest, and strongest, but not subject to imperial dreams. That would be the *Dalou Hegemony* or the *Gloran Empire*.

The *Consensus* existed to keep the peace.

"How soon?" Arya asked as they stopped giggling like wicked school children.

Kaur considered. Again, timing as a weapon she could use, since merchants probably weren't on any schedule and marauders likely were.

"Let's set it for five days from now," she decided. "Time for *Saluki* to fix everything we broke and then pretend like nothing happened. Time for the others to decide if they want to insult me by leaving, or let me *count coup* by staying and attending my court."

"You're even more evil than I am," Ayra accused her, but they were in Kaur's private quarters where Kaur could put aside the severe command officer persona she had to wear outside, and Arya could relax and tell jokes. Their juniors would learn these things eventually.

"That, young lady, is why I am in charge," Kaur replied in an arch voice, just barely suppressing her grin. "Now, go and ruin everybody's day."

The Sub-Commander departed and Kaur reached for her bookreader, but her mind wasn't ready for a mystery thriller, so she put it back down.

One of these days, the *Aditi Consensus* needed to do something about the many places like *Vilahana*, where they skirted all the rules and ethics of polite society, as long as you paid cash up front and didn't ask many questions.

Aranyani couldn't do it herself. Even as part of a larger squadron, with a Ship of the Line or two behind her and the porcupines and wolverines of the Moat in front of her.

What would it take to make the galaxy a better place?

CHAPTER SEVEN

Phil considered the galactic map projected in the air above him as he sat at his station on the flag bridge. He'd asked Heather to come back and sit with him today, just so it was more like the old days. Even on *RAN Cyrus* he hadn't been as isolated from his crew, and after the Academy years he occasionally liked seeing real faces and not just screens.

Everyone else was watching, but Heather here made it more real.

"So according to all our research, the Balhee Cluster is the largest collection of inhabited stars in this gulf," Senior Centurion Sunan Bunnag was saying from her station aboard the survey cruiser *RAN Viking*. "The First Centurion had us run a little ahead of the rest of the squadron. Only enough to confirm things, though. From *Ladaux*, the cluster looks like a solid wall of stars and gases, packed so close together in places that navigation would be complicated. However, several ancient supernovae have opened up most of the interior like a glass-blower working her art. The result is a leaky bowl."

"Leaky?" Phil confirmed.

"That's right, First Centurion," she nodded on her screen. "Sailing notes we've purchased from merchants at home or along the way indicate that the single largest entry point to the interior is at the top of the nebula. There are others, but none of them face anywhere close to us, to the point that we would have to move well inward and around the curve to find one down here."

"What's there?" Phil asked.

He'd read all the reports. Even in this age, all their maps still had a *Here Be Dragons* feel to some of the information. Not as far from home as *Ninagirsu*, where he'd crossed a good chunk of *Aquitaine* and all of *Fribourg* on that sail.

"People," Bunnag replied. "We have indications of various political entities of unknown size, scope, or personality, but we know of the *Yaumgan Domain, Gloran Empire, Dalou Hegemony, Zen-Mekyo Syndicates*, and *Aditi Consensus. Aditi* seems to be the biggest, but fairly deep inside."

"*Aditi?*" Command Centurion Khayriyya Annema spoke up from *Ensenada*. She was senior right now among the Fast Clippers, with *Mexicali* on a run home. "Where do I know that name?"

"In the ancient Hindu religion of Earth, *Aditi* was First Mother," Bunnag said. "Goddess of space, infinity and timelessness. Also a protective Goddess who helps you overcome obstacles. Between that and calling themselves a *Consensus* instead of an Empire or a Hegemony suggests that they might be the most like *Aquitaine*. I would, however, caution anybody against reading too much into that, as some of our notes are a century old at this point and all of you remember what *Fribourg* was like one hundred years ago."

That prompted a round of laughs. Emperor Karl IV. Calling that man a son of a bitch was an insult to dogs everywhere.

Phil reached out and used the controls now to reduce the zoom on the image significantly from where Bunnag had set it. Far enough that this Balhee Cluster looked like a lumpy ball hanging alone in space now, or maybe a confused egg. Closer, or rather behind them at this point, the long galactic arm that contained *Fribourg* and *Aquitaine* looked like a shore on a clear night seen from orbit, a solid run of lights simply tapering off to dark nothingness.

There were stars present. *Urumchi* and her mates had called at a number of them getting this far, but never stayed long. Still, it had taken them four months to cross this distance, and he'd left behind a few ambassadors at small places just to reinforce lines that hadn't frayed over the decades so much as softly faded like an old shirt put through the laundry too many times, with everyone on that busy highway of lights not really looking over here.

"I wanted everyone to notice the distance and more especially the separation between where we are and where we came from," he said, unable to stop himself from dropping into professor voice. That was who he was at this point in his life. *Professor Kosnett.* "First Lord Naoumov could have sent a number of scouts this way before now. However, she was specifically leaving that work for us to do. Additionally, she wanted *Fribourg* to relax, rather than thinking that we were trying to expand around their only open frontier and thus hem them in on that fourth side. The former *Holding of Man* will get their shit together at some point, so we're going this way now."

He paused and looked at faces, realizing that having Heather physically present meant that he felt like he was back on his crazy raid. Maybe he should drag Markus up to sit at the table with him, instead of quietly watching from a corner like Marcelle Travere had always done for Jessica?

"How close are we getting before we set up a more permanent base?" That came from Kaipo Valeriev, Fleet Machinist riding on *CT-9503* and the woman who would take one or both of those bastions off the tug and turn it into their home base, like *The Expedition* had had with Whughy.

"I have reviewed a century's worth of notes," Phil said. "In fact, I taught a course one semester on this frontier that many of your younger officers might have attended. I know many of you audited the class or listened to the recorded lectures. Our tech should have been in advance of theirs, even before Bedrov and Kermode jumped everything forward nearly a century in the last fifteen years."

Phil looked at all the faces on screens. Studied them for clues, but they were all still a little too excited about that next adventure, so he turned to Heather.

"Where would you build?" he asked her.

His tone sounded just like a man giving his students a pop quiz.

But weren't they all?

"We haven't gone vertical yet," Heather noted carefully.

Phil nodded.

"If I was coming out from the inside, I might cut straight across and then take a long glide slope to *Aquitaine* space, so personally, I would ask why you don't drop both here and turn this into a formidable forward operating base?" Heather asked. "All the Clippers can run home immediately, since we'll have a lot of space when we unpack the station, and that sets us up to see how close to that wall we get."

"Do we think there is a gap we might exploit?" Barnaby Silver asked. Command Centurion, *RAN Viking*.

"They always look solid from any distance," Heather said offhand, her eyes taking on that same distant look Phil figured he got when he was back to being a pirate warlord. "The least we can do is check. As Phil said, our tech should be better than theirs, so maybe our sensors and JumpSails will let us do something they can't."

Phil nodded. He grinned as many of the faces around the edges of the screen got quiet and contemplative.

Too many Keller-style warriors with him. He knew that. Not enough long-sailing explorers like Kigali in the fleet, which was again why he wanted Heather in command here and not some fire-breathing berserker like Alber' d'Maine. Not that d'Maine would have been bad. He would have done whatever Phil ordered, but he would have always been looking for a bigger hammer to solve some problems.

Phil wanted an element of sneakiness and surprise.

"That's my thinking as well," Phil said, giving her the gold star. "*RAN Viking* and *RAN Urumchi* will detach from the rest of the squadron after a quick resupply, and then go inspect that wall. Everyone else will remain at Waypoint Twenty-Seven until we return, preparing for the next stage. Questions?"

None, but nobody should be surprised that a former pirate like Phil Kosnett would take an oblique approach to these things, rather than charging at full speed.

He'd done that sort of aggressiveness aboard *CS-405* and *Cyrus* both, and there were times when it was appropriate, but today was not it.

"In that case, everyone start planning for the next major phase of our exploration."

CHAPTER EIGHT

Phil studied the map that they'd bought, projected on his flag bridge screen. Crudely drawn. A child taking a wax pencil and drawing lines roughly separating things into colors. Still, there was a star at the mouth of the tunnel that led deeper into the Cluster.

Viking and *Urumchi* had taken different arcs of the exterior and spent a week exploring. Nothing truly monumental had shown. A few possible gaps were mapped, but none of them had anything on the exterior like waystations or fortresses, so he couldn't tell if the locals knew about them.

So he'd gone up and over, coming straight down, relative to the galactic plane like he'd come from some other galaxy to get here. If they recognized *Aquitaine*, they'd know where he originated. If not, no reason to tell them until they decided to be friendly.

Viking was clear out at the edge of the system, like this was a raid into *Buran* space again. In the old days, when scouts would sit out there and watch. Phil had all the notes from Command Centurion Silver's crew, because they weren't coming on this mission. Similarly, all the Fast Clippers were currently running home, and he expected that *Mexicali* would be back first, while *CT-9503* was staying with the base.

He felt like a primitive war god today. *Urumchi* and seven corvettes. Primed to trade and negotiate. At the same time, Bedrov had designed all these hulls after a lifetime of piracy and war. Then Kermode had upgraded the designs with new weapons.

Phil needed that level of destruction at his fingertips. Not that he intended to unleash it, but scans had detected a large number of ships in orbit of this world. Many of them looked like freighters of various sizes, at least from here. That left a dozen that had the appearance of warships.

None of the hull designs looked like anything he'd ever seen before, assuming that killers tended to be long and lean, rather than boxy, for reasons that had mostly to do with aesthetics.

If they were hostile, Phil might need to defend himself while he extricated the squadron. Or taught the locals some manners. It could go either way. That was why he was in a Survey Dreadnought and not anything lighter. Losing the bubble gun and two of the Type-4s didn't mean he was helpless. There were still the other two, plus twelve Pulse-Two emplacements, three each on the corners for missiles, fighters, and even ships the size of the corvettes around him.

"Countdown?" Phil called.

He had it on the screen in front of him, but he wanted everybody keyed in right now.

"Emergence in three-five seconds," Iveta Beridze replied from the bridge.

She had tactical, but Phil was holding the flag until he knew what the locals would do when faced with a potentially hostile war fleet coming out of jump.

Not too close. In fact, back from the edge of the gravity well far enough that he could maneuver away if he had to without engaging. All of the ships *Viking* had mapped were deep enough that they would have considered themselves safe, but Phil had been there with d'Maine and Aeliaes when they'd charged *Buran* stations and sharks who'd thought being that deep would save them.

Tomorrow's trump card, if Phil needed it.

Emergence.

All of the sensors came live and it was like being back on *CS-405*, since *Urumchi* had comparable systems to go with everything *Viking* had mapped for him.

CC-501 was in line astern, with *CB-502* and *CM-507* holding his front corners and the four guardians aligned behind them but ready to surge forward or hold their own flanks against any surprise.

Too many years at war with *Fribourg*, *Buran*, and even *Salonnia*. But there was no such thing as *too paranoid* in space.

"Send a greeting in all standard languages," Phil called, making eye contact with Harinder now. That was her task. It helped that she'd grown up speaking Hindi natively, in addition to *Aquitaine* English. All the radio traffic they'd picked up was in some variant of Hindi, with a lot of cognates from other languages thrown in. "Confirm everyone's placement against what we knew before."

Orders rattled around. As a minesweeper, *CM-507* has sensors almost as good as *Urumchi*, plus a forward Type-3-Pulse that had been tuned for extremes of range comparable to the old Primaries that used to be the way ships fought each other.

"We've got one hull a little bigger than the old *Founder*-class heavy cruisers in high orbit," Senior Centurion Ekmekçi called from *Urumchi*'s bridge. Science Officer, and one of the best ones available when he'd gone looking. "Battle-tug or something just like it low and forward from them. Most of the other vessels tentatively classified as warships are all close to the cruiser, but do not seem to be escorting it."

"What's the current lag?" Phil asked the room.

"Three seconds round trip," Ekmekçi replied. "We're closing

slowly and they are at rest, so that's not likely to change, but we have no idea where they are in ship's day."

"Maintain heading and stand by for action, but only on my order," Phil reminded everyone.

Little chance of a *Buran*-style surprise, but his standing orders included shooting back with everything anyone had. Only shooting *back*, though.

"Remember, we've probably surprised the hell out of a lot of folks down there."

CHAPTER NINE

Kaur Singh considered the folks around her. Arya had been more successful than either of them had expected, so they'd ended up taking over one of the flight bays and closing it off in order to deploy enough tables for Governor Patte and his entire retinue, plus fourteen other commanders from various ships, each of whom had brought along a handful of their own senior officers to participate in what might be the *Vilahana* social event of the season.

Or something like that.

Aditi Ambassador Trulan was situated with a cluster of pirates along one arm. Arya Chaudhari had another group with her. Kaur had the governor, the commander of *Saluki*, and the rest. No alcohol was being served and nobody was allowed any personal knife longer than their index finger, including two proud, *Gloran* commanders who had objected loudly, then shut up when Kaur's combat teams looked like they might just open fire.

Kaur suspected they were just putting on a performance for the galleries, rather than being actually offended that they might be disarmed. Every Sikh here had a blade, but they were all shorter than the allowed limit. Culture, rather than dueling.

Dinner had been mostly a success, and now everyone was having keer or some other dessert.

"So, Commander," Governor Patte smiled over his sweet rice now. "Will I be granted any satisfaction for my complaints about your behavior?"

Kaur didn't take the man seriously. From the smile on his face, she wondered if he considered such conversation some bizarre form of foreplay. Still, she could engage in mind games with the man.

"You are quiet welcome to accompany me to the nearest *Aditi* Fleet Base, Governor," she smiled back. "From there, you should be able to hire transport to a civilian system with a *Consensus* court that might decide it has jurisdiction to let you file a formal case before it."

And pigs might fly.

She studied the man.

"Should I have my crew vacate a cabin for you?" Kaur continued. "You could take one aide with you, as those cabins are usually set up with two bunks stacked."

The sourness that filled his eyes warmed her soul, but *Vilahana* was a pirate base by any measure you wished to use. Not in *Aditi* space. Not subject to *Aditi* rules. Nothing she could do about it except show up with a big enough hammer to make everyone behave while she was here.

Tomorrow, the day after at the latest, they would go back to being smugglers and rogues.

Kaur happened to be looking in the right direction when one of her security team members suddenly perked up, nodded, and started towards her at a not-quite-jogging pace, so she shut up now and ignored everyone around her. They picked up that something had changed.

Even Governor Patte refrained from baiting or propositioning her.

The woman stepped close and handed her a headset comm she'd pulled from a pocket on her armor.

"Singh," Kaur said into the comm.

"Nagarkar," Namrata replied instantly. "We have a situation."

"Go ahead."

"An entire squadron of what look like warships just came out of jump at the edge of the well," Namrata said. "They are hailing everyone in formal Hindi and awaiting an answer."

"Confirm scale?" Kaur asked, not telling everyone around her just yet.

"One monster bigger than us plus seven escorts, except they are surrounding the Line Ship instead of phalanxing in front of it," Namrata said.

"Formal Hindi?" Kaur pressed.

"Straight out of a book, Commander, rather than how we speak," Namrata said with some levity in her voice now. "Horrible accents, too, so I'm guessing we're dealing with an alien invasion."

Kaur nodded to herself.

In spite of ten thousand or more years of space flight, nobody had ever encountered any advanced life form other than Humans. Alien meant someone from outside the cluster.

Who knew what those people were about?

Kaur left the headset in place but focused her attention on the governor now. He'd only gotten the weak half of the conversation, but the man had gone pale anyway, like maybe he was a mind reader.

"May I have your attention, please?" Kaur called to the room, rather than yelling at everyone to fall silent and listen.

Arya took up the call as well. Eventually, everyone did shut up.

"Many of you might be getting messages shortly from your own vessels," Kaur said. "It appears a squadron of eight unknown vessels has just arrived in-system and wants to talk."

She was staring at Patte by the time she finished. Kaur could already see heads turning to the other flight deck, but she'd originally sent her shuttles out to gather everyone, rather than let pirates land on her decks, so they were all trapped here for the time being.

"What are you going to do?" Patte demanded quietly.

Kaur smiled, then turned to let that cover all the officers and commanders around her.

"I intend to go see what they want," she said. "Would anyone care to come with me?"

CHAPTER TEN

Phil studied the maneuver plot that the largest ship down there had assumed.

There had been a flurry of radio traffic, most of it scrambled, between that vessel and the ones around it, followed by three shuttles launching in quick order. One of those had run like mad for the battle-tug in low orbit, while the other two seemed to be making least-course circuits to the fourteen smaller ships in orbit.

Had he caught them in the middle of a cocktail party or something equally silly?

"Target *Alpha* identifies as *Aditi Consensus* Cruiser *Aranyani*," Leyla Ekmekçi announced over the general comm. "The big tug is flying local colors as a *Vilahana* ship, as are two of the others. The rest are a mix of places. Nobody seems to be maneuvering to keep up with *Aranyani*."

Phil chewed on that for a long second. Multi-nation squadrons usually required a lot of cross-training, which was why *Fribourg* had originally asked for and hired *First Expeditionary Fleet* as a unit for their far border. All Jessica's people, plus people trained to *her* standards and culture.

"Is *Aranyani* showing them a tail, or slipping to a flank as it maneuvers?" Phil asked, studying the vectors.

"Looks like a side-slip or three in progress, First Centurion," came the answer.

Phil nodded. Well-met strangers rather than trusted allies. *Aranyani* was coming out to talk, and the others were hanging back to see if they should run, rather than scrambling to defend the system.

"Hail *Aranyani* directly on a narrow laser," Phil ordered. "Connect everyone at our end with the same silent network."

Just like the old days as a pirate. Lasers would give some flash of light off hulls, but nothing like using general comms and trusting the encryption.

"I have *Aranyani* on channel three," Harinder replied after a moment. "The signal is a little messy and choppy. They might not be used to doing this. One second lag each way."

One second? Good enough. That made you stop and listen politely, instead of bulling ahead. Made you compress everything into discrete chunks instead of meandering when you talked.

They would know who he was quickly enough, but that just gave them a direction to sail. His forward base was off in a corner they'd have to be struck by lightning to find right now.

"This is the *Republic of Aquitaine* vessel *Urumchi*," Phil said. "First Centurion Philip Kosnett commanding. To whom do I have the pleasure of talking?"

He left it at that. Unless they had weapons like his, he was out of range of them doing anything right now. And hadn't threatened anybody. Hopefully, he was dealing with civilized folk.

Of course, *Buran* had considered itself civilized, but had still been intent on conquering the entire universe until *First Expeditionary* and Lady Moirrey had done something about it.

A female face appeared. South Asian, using the ancient geographic locations from *Lost Earth*. Dark skin not nearly as red as the Hispanic that was common in *Aquitaine*. Dark hair. Dark eyes.

Phil guessed her to be about his age, so mid-forties, give or take. She had a face used to commanding naval warships. That left marks.

"I am Commander Kaur Singh of the *Aditi Consensus* Cruiser *Aranyani*," she said, her accent hard to follow. "What is your purpose here, *Urumchi*?"

She paused. Light second gaps made conversations stilted, but she was apparently used to it as well.

"Trade and exploration, *Aranyani*," Phil said. "We have crossed the gulf from your east to see what is out here."

Heather's light came on, so Phil looked at her and locked the channel to the other ship briefly.

"What's up, Heather?" he asked.

"All of the other ships are starting to spread out, Phil," she said. "No serious blueshift or redshift yet, but I've been watching silhouettes and everyone seems to be riding their gyros right now, turning away from us."

"Match up national flags with our maps and confirm where you think they're headed," Phil said.

"Roger that."

Phil turned back to Commander Singh.

"*Vilahana* is not part of any larger political entity, *Urumchi*," she was saying. "If you seek trade, I would invite you to accompany us back to *Aditi* itself. My mission here was to rescue a vessel captured by pirates, which I have completed, and now I was headed inward."

Inward?

Phil considered what terms you might use to navigate inside a hollow sphere. *Vilahana* was at the mouth of a balloon that would not deflate. Or the opening of a large bottle.

"Thank you for the invitation, *Aranyani*," Phil said. "But as we are strangers just coming to this part of the galaxy, I should probably call on the local governing body. It is my expectation that trade from *Aquitaine* is likely to pass through this system, so we plan to establish diplomatic relations against future need."

Harinder typed something on her screen that popped up on his as a scrolling marquee now.

-Aranyani was here rescuing someone from pirates? Are we in danger from the locals?-

Phil caught her eye above the camera focused on him and nodded. He didn't know.

Another message appeared. Heather.

-Phil, I have a Governor Annen Patte on a separate line, trying to reach you. Seems to be local executive.-

Phil considered all the repercussions of his appearance, especially if an *Aditi* vessel was here on a military mission, and intending to depart.

##-Have him hold for now-##

"Very well, *Urumchi*," Kaur Singh said after the gap. "We will remain for a time so we can meet in person. Welcome."

"She just cut from her end," Harinder said aloud.

"Bring up the Governor then," Phil replied. "What's my lag to him?"

"One point five," she said. "He seems to be aboard the battle-tug. Broadcasting wide and unscrambled. Maybe he was aboard *Aranyani* and that shuttle took him when we got here?"

"Most likely scenario, Harinder," Phil nodded.

"You're live," she replied.

"Greetings, Governor Patte," he said. "I am *Aquitaine* First Centurion Kosnett, aboard *RAN Urumchi*. We have come to establish diplomatic relations with the many nations of the Balhee Cluster."

There, let him know that he was just one player in a larger whole. Phil suspected that the man might not be entirely on the up and up. Especially given the spaces in orbit that looked like nothing so much as junkyards. Hundreds of signals reflecting passively from his scanners, some of which looked like whole ships slowly tumbling, so Phil and everyone had assumed they were being stripped. Or an orbital junkyard.

Still, he'd spent enough time around Keller's various people to understand what the limits of the law might be in places where the writ ran thin.

"Greetings, *Aquitaine*!" the man spoke now. "We are most excited to make your acquaintance and look forward to hosting you! I am Governor Patte and it is my fervent hope that we can both become fantastically wealthy via trade! I am currently aboard one of my vessels, having been aboard *Aranyani* when you arrived, but nothing less would do than to welcome you on the surface at my palace, where we can treat you right!"

Phil was already growing tired of the number of exclamation points the man apparently spoke with, but that was an occasional hazard of the job. Governors in many places were elected or appointed politicians with glad hands. At least Phil had highly-trained ambassadors along that he could foist off on the man for now. It still sounded like the *Aditi Consensus* would be the place to start.

"Thank you, Governor," Phil concluded. "I will have my staff work with yours to make arrangements for everything."

And cut.

Phil released a sigh and located Heather's image in his group of Command Centurions.

"Let me know who breaks for home and who stays put, Heather," Phil said. "And keep a list of them against future encounters. I'm expecting to send Silver and *Viking* deeper, once we know what we're facing, but most of the squadron will remain with us."

"Understood, Phil," she said.

Phil turned to everyone and nodded at the faces, both on his screen and around the room.

"Okay, team, we have made first contact," he said. "From here it gets a little more interesting, but hopefully pretty boring, pretty fast. Harinder, you and Fleet Ambassador Babatunde figure out who we'll leave behind as our contact, along with their embassy, so we can drag both along to whatever meetings are on the ground. We'll be here longer than previous stops, because we're going to have to establish ground rules for things, and I'm sure everyone that runs for home now probably brings back their own ambassador or contact when they return. Pay attention to those vessels as they show up. I'll end up on the ground at some point, but Heather will be up here and anybody who starts anything will us ends up facing everyone. Same rules as always, except that now we're operating on the thinner margin, so plan accordingly. I won't ask if you have questions, because I don't have answers. Route everything to Harinder for now and we'll go from there. Dismissed."

He cut the line and rubbed the bridge of his nose. This felt like the opening gambit in a much more complicated game than anyone back home might have anticipated. That was why Pet had selected him for it four years ago.

He had not been slacking those days away, getting ready.

Hopefully the people of the Cluster were ready for him.

CHAPTER ELEVEN

Looking around the reception hall, Kaur didn't like it, but there was nothing at all she could do about the situation.

Governor Patte had mousetrapped her perfectly. Whether he'd meant to or it had been an accident the man would never admit either way, but she had no doubts. At least she had been able to escort the freighter until it reached Jump and vanished, with secret instructions to head to the second-closest naval base before they did anything else. Second-closest because those damned pirates might decide to park close to the nearest one, hunting.

Right now, she was on the surface of *Vilahana*, but she'd at least pulled a fast one on Patte, coming down in a mere shuttle instead of riding the entire boom section of *Aranyani*, like everyone else probably expected. The landing field had been littered with various booms as almost everyone else was flying in vessels too small to have a dedicated flight bay.

The strangers didn't do a boom separation into two pieces, weird as that was. *Urumchi* was one vessel, rather than boom and engine like other people did it.

How the hell did they haul cargo around? In those tiny shuttle craft?

She sighed as she went slowly through the Governor's receiving line. Too much to learn.

Aditi Consensus Ambassador Trulan had been shanghaied again, except by Kaur this time, and turned loose on the strangers. Trulan was a paunchy, gray bureaucrat who seemed to never speak above a superior cattiness appropriate to a bridge table. Kaur didn't expect much, but the *Consensus* needed him here more than *Troeg* right now.

Because he was a diplomat, trained specifically for this sort of thing, while Kaur Singh was a Commander. Though she was called upon frequently to conduct diplomacy in strange places, she still felt better turning things over to a professional. Better, when this supposed First Centurion, whatever that was, had also brought diplomatic underlings on his mission.

It brought a useful symmetry that Kaur wanted to use to her benefit.

Trulan was done with the Governor, exchanging inanities. He moved on and Kaur found herself facing Patte. He was shorter than she remembered, but he had such a large personality that it took her a moment to recall that she was still taller than he was.

"Ah, Commander," Patte said in a grand voice suddenly booming across the room. "So glad that you were able to visit my palace after all!"

"Wouldn't have missed it for anything, Governor Patte," she replied politely.

It was true. They would have needed tractors to drag her away from meeting an ambassador/commander from the fabled ancient lands of *Aquitaine*. Baudin had come from there, the man who had invented the modern JumpSail and made it possible to get around the cluster easily.

Occasionally, Kaur read historical books set in the earlier Renaissance, when humanity had first returned to the stars after the long hiatus. She could only imagine what those sailors a thousand years ago had done. And to get here from either galactic arm boggled the mind.

"So, Commander Singh," Patte continued to boom. "As you have an ambassador to leave with me, I presume that this means the *Consensus* will be interested in upgrading their relations with *Vilahana*?"

Kaur nodded and kept her mouth shut for a long moment. In the background, Trulan had turned even more gray and his eyes looked like a large vehicle had just come around a curve, finding him in the middle of an icy road.

"As you know, Governor, my mission here was strictly military and constabulary in nature," Kaur finally said. "Dealing with some folks who obviously neglected to mention to you that they had captured the freighter and cargo that they were planning to sell. It seems to be a common failing, and one you might wish to review with your customs officials at some future date. Right now however, I presume that Ambassador Trulan will have all those answers for you. I myself am merely present for the novelty of meeting folks from the ancient home of the modern age."

Patte blinked as he processed her words. Probably expecting her to be a muscle-head berserker. Commanders of smaller boats were like that because they were generally assigned to a hot spot in the phalanx. Only the heavy cruisers were well-rounded and well-armed enough to take care of themselves without the other lines around them, so the *Consensus* made sure that they had Commanders ready for this sort of silliness.

Patte looked like he was winding himself up for a loquacious retort, but she was saved by the arrival of the strangers. Their entry preceded them like a wavefront, dropping a wall of silence that raced outward and engulfed everyone.

Governor Patte broke formation and began walking directly towards them, ignoring everyone he was supposed to talk to yet. Probably didn't want anyone getting in on a deal without him.

Kaur followed, her longer legs allowing her to stay right in his pocket, inside his own team of bodyguards with her combat team and Ambassador Trulan trailing a bit outside that.

Kosnett was tall. Half a head taller than her. Maybe a full head above Patte. His uniform was stretched tight over a strong frame, unlike her own that was more baggy and loose.

Aquitaine colors were black and green, with five stripes on the man's upper right arm and a patch on his left shoulder. Others wore something identical, but only had three or fewer stripes. There was one woman with him that had four stripes, but she didn't project an air of the warrior like Kosnett and most of the others did.

Patte was wearing a simple black outfit for this meeting, long robes presumably over matching pants and a pale blue shirt, like usual when he wasn't wearing a blazer. Kaur was in her better day uniform, but Patte had specifically called this a casual meet and greet, with a state dinner to be scheduled for a later date.

Kaur smiled at all the poor pirates trapped here and unable to get into trouble without getting into trouble. Only five ships had left, presumably running like hell for home. Given relative flight times, that meant either a *Gloran* or *Dalou* representative would probably arrive first, with her own help a distant third.

She had no idea how long it might be for an *Ewin Principality* king or duke to get the news and come see. And nobody was ever sure what might cause the *Yaumgan* to emerge from their philosophical slumbers.

Patte came to a stop in front of the *Aquitaine* party. His bodyguards were more wound up than Kosnett's, while still looking less professional. But then, Patte just had to worry about assassins. Kosnett might have chosen his combat team for storming hostile planets. They gave off a quiet whiff of readiness to do just that.

Kaur approved and gave her own people a signal to relax several degrees. Let Patte provoke an incident with the strangers.

"First Centurion Kosnett, so exciting to make your

acquaintance!" Patte boomed over the entire audience. Like normal.

Kosnett did a polite half-bow and gestured to the man on his right, with three stripes on his arm. Kaur studied the woman standing a step back and between them as the man spoke. She was African ethnotype, dark skinned and with curly ringlets starting to come in gray. Utterly gorgeous, and Kaur didn't even fancy women all that much. But she had sharp eyes marking everyone and everything that happened in front of her, even closer than Kosnett's combat team.

"Governor Patte, allow me to introduce you to Command Diplomatic Centurion Ikram Wattana," Kosnett said, indicating the three stripe.

Command Diplomatic Centurion? What an interesting rank. It suggested that the man was in *Aquitaine*'s navy, rather than being a civilian.

Wattana himself appeared to be an Arabic ethnotype, lighter in skin than the four stripe but still darker than Kosnett. How wide a range of ethnologies did *Aquitaine* represent? The Cluster tended towards the South Asian, as Earth had once called them, with small fractions of most of the rest of the home planet.

"Pleasure, Governor," Wattana matched the bow Kosnett had given, so presumably what they thought adequate to the rank of piratical bureaucratic overlord of a planet.

Kaur suppressed her grin at Patte's new title, at least the one she was going to remember.

Kosnett's party seemed to be those three, with the rest a scattering of combat team in armor and ready for an attack that they would demolish, from the gleams in the eyes she could see.

Kosnett turned to her and smiled.

"Commander Singh," he called across the slight space, matching the bow Patte had gotten.

Kaur reciprocated it so nobody could see the sudden grin that was there and then gone again.

"First Centurion Kosnett," Kaur replied a moment later,

taking the opportunity to step right up next to a squat killer in black and green, who immediately slid sideways exactly enough that he wouldn't touch her flesh or cloth if she didn't move. But still close enough to tackle her instantly if she drew a weapon. "Welcome to *Vilahana* and the Balhee Cluster. How may we be of service?"

CHAPTER TWELVE

Phil studied the tall woman representing the *Aditi Consensus* and possibly-only-accidentally upstaging the governor. He had the impression that she didn't think too highly of the man. Given that he might be running a galactic chop shop from the junkyards *Urumchi* and *Viking* had scanned from orbit, Phil might tend to agree with her.

But that also opened the way to trade. Lots of it, if no single political entity controlled the system best suited to accessing the inner cluster. JumpSails would allow you to go anywhere, but being able to set up a merchant node here saved a lot of travel time back and forth, because you could positively race across that emptiness of the gulf, with hardly any density slowing you down.

"I come as an explorer," Phil replied, mostly to the woman, but pointedly including the short governor in his words. "I have, however, also brought with me a number of credentialed ambassadors from *Aquitaine* so that we can establish all manner of diplomatic and trade ties between nations of the Cluster and *Aquitaine*, as well as governments on my side of the gulf, such as the *Fribourg Empire, Lincolnshire, Salonnia,* and even *Corynthe.*"

It was educational, watching eyes glaze over a little as he

named places that were probably mere legends this far away. *Fribourg* they might have heard of. The others were doubtful. Phil was okay with that.

Probably be rude, asking for legal permission to set up a duty free transfer station in orbit, and letting rent and increased trade cover the bills. Or not. Patte looked like a man with a finger in every cookie jar.

Wattana's problem. Not anything Phil had to deal with. Not yet, anyway.

And Patte caught the reference to *nations of the cluster*, as did Singh. The former bristled, just a little. The latter smiled.

We're here to talk to everyone, Sri.

"Explorer?" Singh spoke up before the governor could. "Where are you headed from here?"

"We have long known that the Balhee Cluster was inhabited," Phil said. "It was the vast distance and the few stars between that limited contact. However, the long period of wars that had been in existence are now over, so *Aquitaine* can trade."

"Who won?" Singh asked bluntly.

But she looked and acted like a Command Centurion off a Heavy Cruiser, the ships that the First Lord sent out to do errands, when a full battle fleet wasn't necessarily called for.

Necessarily.

"Humanity, Commander Kaur," Phil replied, maybe a little sharper than necessary. "*Aquitaine* was able to convince the *Fribourg Empire* to accept and honor a broad and profitable peace. *Fribourg* even asked *Aquitaine* to help them fight *Buran*, a nation of the interior that had been ruled for millennia by one of the ancient *Sentiences* that had assumed a mission to conquer the entire galaxy and remake it. I was part of that fleet. The Emperor of *Fribourg* and her Consort are old friends and both sent me presents before I departed in this mission. Blessings on the trip, as it were. We are at peace. Trade and friendship with strangers was the next logical step."

Again, that blink of shock as they processed his words.

Whole megawars being fought in the wider galaxy that they knew nothing about, surrounded by the great nebula and mostly isolated by it. Phil could only imagine what a shark fleet would have done dropping out of Jump and announcing a new galactic order to these folks in another century or three.

And maybe it was stretching things a little to call Karl VIII a friend, but he had sat in meetings with Centurion *zu* Weigand. Arlo had few true friends, but he wouldn't have sent a telescope except as a peace offering for their nearly-deadly encounter at *Hemera*. Phil would count that.

"We have much to learn," Singh said gravely after a beat.

Then she nodded to him, turned to the governor, and bowed again.

It took the man a half-second to regain his momentum. Then it was like a light bulb came on in his eyes.

"Come, my friends!" he said, stepping forward to take Wattana's arm in his own and drawing the Command Centurion out of Phil's orbit. So to speak. "Let us celebrate new friendships! Wine? Whiskey? What will you have?"

"With your permission, of course, Governor, we have brought some things with us," Phil countered. "While we have all had our various vaccinations, we thought it would be safer for everyone if our first such meeting didn't end with someone suffering a bout of gastrointestinal issues, so we have juice we brought from my flagship."

He nodded to Markus, wearing his new insulated backpack, who immediately walked close and turned his back. Phil reached a hand in and grabbed two bottles, handing one to Wattana and keeping one for himself.

Keller had taught him that trick a long time ago. Never accept drinks from strangers. And only drink alcohol sparingly in events such as this. A number of men and women around the room had belt knives, reminding him of Bedrov and other pirates from *Corynthe* that he had known. Only *Pops* Nakamura had never bothered to walk around armed, but everybody respected *Pops*.

Patte seemed a bit deflected, but still started dragging the larger group over to what was obviously a bar, as bystanders and pedestrians panicked a little at the oncoming horde and fled to the wings. Patte looked like the kind of man who would be charging for things, but Phil didn't let that stop him from paying close attention as Patte and Singh both ordered.

The Governor had whiskey. Singh ordered a glass of wine that required the woman on the other side of the bar to open a new bottle. Whether that was taste or care on her part Phil couldn't say. Maybe she'd taken his example to heart?

Around them, all the other folks hovered. That was the term for it. Not like pissy hummingbirds or anything. Nervous mice ready to scamper into the high grass at the first warning, maybe.

Of course, the biggest of those other warships in orbit were less than twice as big as one of Phil's corvettes. Old style destroyers like *Aquitaine* had been building as recently as fifteen years ago. *Aranyani* had been queen of the battlefield, right up to the moment *Urumchi* arrived. Only the battle-tug came close, in terms of total displacement.

But this was a First Contact with alien cultures. And there were any number of other places that Phil and Fleet Ambassador Aliza Babatunde needed to visit. Nothing much would be accomplished here, other than meeting folks and adjusting his accent to be a little more clipped and precise than it had been back home.

He took a sip of his orange juice and let the crowd begin to circulate again.

CHAPTER THIRTEEN

Heather studied the readout but couldn't make heads or tails of it. She looked around the bridge once, mostly to orient from her screen.

"Leyla, what am I seeing with *Aranyani* and the others?" she asked, causing her Science Officer to pop up from her own focus.

"Boss?"

"*Aranyani*," Heather prompted. "Naval architecture."

"Think *Buran*, boss," Leyla said now, brushing her long, wavy, black hair back out of her eyes. Gray eyes. Sharp ones that never missed anything. "These ships all look to be designed to separate into two sections, just like the sharks did. *Buran, Energiya*."

"Why didn't *Aranyani*?" Heather asked. "Educate me on that one."

"Dunno why, when everyone else split off their front third or maybe half," Leyla continued now. "Pretty sure I've identified where it would split, but won't know until they do."

"Oh?"

"So you look at the *Aditi* ship from above, and it looks kinda like a fist with three fingers stuck out of the front," Leyla said.

After a moment, she keyed her console and took over the main screen, as well as letting anyone else on the bridge, or even flag that was paying attention, listen in. "Middle finger is twice as long and thick as the other two. Think all of that and part of where it sockets into the fist will come loose. Maybe a good chunk of the centerline core. They haven't gone bow-on to us except at first, but I have scans showing some sort of heavy weapon mount on the center spine, and four smaller ones, paired on the outer fingers. Then things that look like beam emplacements, five of them, seem to cover all the approaches without focusing anywhere. Smaller ones in pairs seem to be forward and both flanks."

"Five Type-3 and six Type-1, maybe?" Heather asked, seeing that design architecture in her head, now that Leyla was pointing at things.

"Yeah, maybe, but I'd have to see them fire to know," Leyla replied. "That thing on the centerline concerns me."

"Why?" Heather asked bluntly.

"So we're only seeing one ship that came out of an *Aditi Consensus* yard, boss." Leyla clicked a button and more than a dozen ships were all displayed, the smaller ones scaled up to appear the same size as the big one. She highlighted one set. "All of this group has a thick, stubby central spine, and what look like paired engines out on pylons, rather than snugged up against the hull. They kinda look like space dragons, if you squint real hard. That central piece separates and takes the top half of the rear section with them."

Another group got highlighted now.

"These folks have a long, skinny lighthouse stuck out, and the same sort of engine array, but those pylons are much shorter and angled down. The secondary hull, what we might call *Energiya*, is pretty flat across the front, and looks like a lot of beam emplacements out on those forward corners, covering forward and flank, almost like castles on a chess board, if you would."

"What about this last guy?" Heather asked, indicating the one left over.

"Weirdest of the group, Commander," Leyla shrugged. "Hexagonal column on its side, with the front tucked into the back just like the sharks did it, but not that many beams. Looks like a metric shit-ton of lateral missile launchers, though. Like the old *Homeworld*-class missile cruisers."

Heather remembered those. Keller had taken *Ishfahan* on her first invasion of *Fribourg*, but left them behind against *Buran*. The ability to short-jump out of a missile's path rendered them irrelevant as weapons.

"Any chance they have Capriole drives?" Heather asked.

"That is exactly what I've been trying to figure out for the last six hours, Heather," Leyla replied. "They don't act like *Sentient* ships, and we've got all sorts of notes from your old adventures. But it looks like they grabbed our JumpSails and retrofitted them onto their hulls without taking most of our weapons. Plus, nobody but us mounts Type-4s on a warship. Or bubble guns."

"Could that heavy on the central spine of *Aranyani* be something like a bubble gun?" Heather asked.

"Huh, hadn't thought of that," Leyla replied. "Not a big enough port, but maybe a scaled down version? Keep the blaster part and skip the double-hand slap?"

"That cruiser looks like it was designed to sit right in the middle of combat, Leyla," Heather noted. "Surrounded on all sides like we are, but maybe part of some sort of echelon formation instead of rings. Firing beams at flanks while pounding someone bow-on to them. What about the others?"

"Hard to separate *Dalou* from *Gloran*," Leyla said. "Maybe *Dalou* is selling old hulls to *Gloran*, because I have two ships out there both flying *Gloran Empire* transponders, and one of them looks like a cheap knock-off of the only *Dalou* still around."

"Assume old alliances and maybe technology transfers," Heather said. "*Aquitaine* and *Lincolnshire*, before things got weird there at the end with Keller and *Lincolnshire* split off from their close alliance with us."

"Yeah, that would hold water," Leyla said. "One thing's sure, though. I got no idea what they are going to be like in combat."

"What's *Aranyani's* power curve relative to a *Founder*-class?" Heather asked.

Those had been the workhorse of the Navy before Bedrov designed the Expeditionary Cruisers to replace them. To replace everything.

"Down maybe ten percent, if they had everything on and running when they sailed out to say hi to us that first time," Leyla replied after looking something up.

Ten percent?

"Match for the old *City*-class boats?" Heather asked. "The old light cruisers like *Hualien*?"

"Yeah," Leyla agreed. "Bigger hull than *Hualien*, but a *Founder* could probably take her head-on in an arena fight. Be close. *Viking* could kick her ass, as long as they stayed out at a distance and hammered her with the Fours. We'd stomp her into the mud at just about any range, unless she brought a lot of friends to the yard."

Heather nodded. She and Phil had talked about the possible technology variances at play. *Aquitaine* had been fighting a war with *Fribourg* for nearly two centuries, off and on. That pushed ships and technology. Then *Buran* forced everyone a big jump forward at once. These later designs—*Urumchi*, *Viking*, and the *Scorpion*-class corvettes around her—were all built with lessons from the *Buran* war, many of them learned from her old home *CS-405*.

The Balhee Cluster was an isolated environment that might not have had access to advances in naval architecture, which was why Phil had been willing to travel in an undergunned Survey Dreadnought instead of one of the big combat monsters that First Lord was building these days.

But it was Heather's job to make sure that those assumptions held.

"New standing order," Heather called out, making sure everyone stopped typing and looked up as she formulated the words. "Every six hours, like clockwork, *Urumchi* will hard scan everything nearby. *Viking* and *CM-507* will be listening on passive, but neither vessel will do the same without a good reason, as we don't want to give away too much. Whole squadron will share everything they pick up, and make sure everyone is listening. We'll do the first one in forty-three minutes at the top of the hour, so let them know."

"On it," Leyla replied, typing furiously now.

Heather wasn't afraid of *Aranyani*. Even if everyone else joined that cruiser for an attack. The corvettes could hold them off and *Urumchi* had been designed with the sharks in mind.

It would be when they wanted to start a grand promenade that would get interesting. Heather had no doubts that some of the ships that had left were likely to return with friends. Maybe squadrons.

Then, things might be a little more messy.

CHAPTER FOURTEEN

Phil looked up from his report when the door to his day office opened and Harinder stuck her head in.

"You're being hailed, First Centurion," she said in an innocent voice that still sounded like it was up to no good.

"By?"

"Kaur Singh off *Aranyani*," Harinder nodded.

He nodded and rose. Phil had wondered how long it would take for the *Aditi Consensus* to reach out directly.

"I'll take it out there," he said, moving to join her. "Wake Heather, Iveta, and Aliza up and have them listen in."

"Got it," she said as she moved to her station.

Phil settled across the round table from Harinder and ran his hands through his hair once, just to make sure it looked presentable. Almost time to get it cut again, but he'd been busy with paperwork before they'd arrived and Markus had forgotten to drag him to the barber.

"Coming live in three, two, one…" Harinder said.

Commander Kaur Singh appeared in the big three-dimensional projection, facing him from the middle of the table, twice normal size.

"Good afternoon, Commander," Phil welcomed her. "To what do I owe the pleasure?"

He studied her face. They had managed a few semi-private conversations while he was on the ground, but Governor Patte had sought to monopolize his time. For all the obvious reasons.

That man could smell all the levs of trade that Phil was bringing with him. And really did seem to have his fingers in every cookie jar.

"It was my hope that you would be interested in a tour of *Aranyani*, First Centurion," she said. "My officers have been studying your vessel, but it is so radically alien that they aren't entirely sure what they see, so I suspect your folks have the same issue."

"Won't your spies get upset if we steal each other's secrets before they have a chance?" Phil asked with a grin.

"Possibly, but that's a risk I'm willing to take, given the long lead time before such lazy creatures could even make it here from *Aditi*," she grinned back.

Phil liked her. She had an easy way with command and a solid grasp of information and details. Many of the other command centurions at that soiree had looked to Phil like pirates, but they hadn't come up from the ranks like folks in *Corynthe* did.

Duels with knives, as it were, left a man or woman much more focused than they had been. Most of the locals were probably just smugglers with guns.

And *Vilahana* really did remind Phil of a chop shop.

"How soon do you expect reinforcements, Commander?" Phil asked, wondering just how far he might take this conversation.

From what he understood, it would be one hell of a sail for a squadron from *Aditi*, but not impossible. The Cluster enforced certain flight restrictions, so he had the impression that most ships weren't meant for the sorts of long-sailing missions that Tomas Kigali still did in his spare time as a civilian.

Singh shrugged in the projection.

"It will take time for that freighter to make the run," she said. "Then to convince a Director that they aren't hysterical. Finally, they would have to assemble something from scratch and sail here. I expect to be on my own for at least a month, depending on your itinerary."

Phil was impressed. First Lord could have reacted faster, but she was a veteran of both wars, and used to moving ships and fleets around.

"So you think we should wait here?" Phil asked. "Make sure your superiors have time to react appropriately?"

"I think that *Dalou* and *Gloran* squadrons will arrive before then," she countered. "Only the *Ewin Princes* and possibly *Yaumgan* will not arrive before my friends back home. Vishnu knows we already have representatives of several representatives of the *Zen-Mekyo Syndicates* here, and that's only going to get worse."

"Ah," Phil replied. "Perhaps we should schedule another event like the one on the ground, but I should hold it aboard *Urumchi*, then? Set it several weeks out and give everyone a chance to attend?"

She wasn't fast enough to hide the spike of either fear or anger that lit up her eyes for a moment. It helped that her eyes were twice as big as normal, so they really lit up.

But she also got it under control faster than he had expected.

"That would certainly be one way to make sure you were well acquainted with everyone," she replied carefully. "But I had originally called to see about inviting you aboard *Aranyani*, First Centurion."

"Indeed, you did," Phil said graciously. "Let me talk to my staff and have them work with yours to arrange a time. I have adjusted my ship clock to the sun over the governor's palace, so we are a few hours ahead of our nominal dinner time. Would tomorrow be too soon?"

Again, she had the slightest flinch, but Phil was the only

player at the table right now who had spent years planning out these scenarios. Gaming every possibility in his head, then spare time with his wife and friends. Walking his various students through them as classroom assignments, and letting those minds turn in term papers exploring various facets of first contact.

"No, First Centurion," Singh said. "That would be lovely. I will have my staff contact yours and make arrangements."

"Thank you," Phil said.

And she was gone.

Phil drew a heavy breath and released it. The *Aditi Consensus* was the biggest player, as near as everyone agreed. Non-expansionist, but playing something of a role as galactic cop to the many colonies and systems of the cluster that weren't strongly associated with the others.

"Okay, gang, thoughts?" he asked the aether.

"Should you take Iveta?" Heather asked first. "That puts my Tactical Officer on their bridge to ask innocent questions."

Innocent. Sure. Phil wasn't fooled.

"Phil, were you serious about having a reception here?" Aliza asked.

"I was," he said, replying to the second question and putting the first one on hold for a bit. "If that many players are going to be represented, it puts us in a position that all your ambassadors can start meeting people and making connections. We'll need that later, and can start feeling out trade treaties. I'd like to see about *Vilahana* as a base of some sort, but suspect that they have a reputation to overcome."

"What gave it away?" Heather laughed. "Junk yards and minefields?"

"Minefields?" Phil paused.

"Each of those junkyards are surrounded by marker beacons," Heather said. "Perimeter claims. Everything bigger than a coffin is also broadcasting a transponder with ownership. There are minefields around a lot of things, including many of the stations and most of the important-looking wrecks."

"We're sure they are mines?" Phil asked.

That hadn't come up yet, but they'd only been here long enough to start asking questions. Not learning secrets.

"That's the consensus, looking at the scan returns," Heather said. "About two thirds explosive and one third that look like those old archerfish missiles, firing a beam of some sort. Ships are extremely careful when they fly around here, at least when they get high enough above the surface where most people would normally relax. No-go zones."

"Interesting," Phil noted. "Make sure Isabèl Pan and *CM-507* are on top of that."

"Oh, they are, Phil," Heather laughed. "Her folks were the ones that noted it first and let me know."

"So tomorrow," he said. "Are we prepared to have the Tactical Officer off the ship if something happens?"

He caught a hint of disappointment under someone's breath. Probably Beridze, afraid she might miss something. You have to make a choice.

"*Viking* is nearby if anybody starts anything," Heather said. "And I'll let Galia Abbasi and Erle Kuiper know so *CC-501* and *CB-502* are ready to engage on short notice."

"Very well," he said. "Aliza, you start planning for something big. Work with Rei Bottenberg on a menu. They have the best feel for that sort of thing of any Wardroom centurion I've ever worked with, and find cooking for people the highest form of love."

"Understood, Phil," the Fleet Ambassador replied.

"Iveta, plan for a half-day," Phil decided. "Heather and Aliza figure out morning or afternoon, but not both for this visit. We'll invite her next week for a matching tour here, so warn Sergey that I intend to show him off."

"He's likely to pot strawberries for her to take home," Heather replied with a laugh.

"Whatever form diplomacy needs to take," Phil said. "That's part of the reason I brought the man. Legends of the old *Science*

Officer, Javier Aritza himself, and all the Johnny Appleseed things that ancient did, as it were. Questions?"

Silence.

He brought his focus to the woman across the table from him.

"Harinder, you'll be with me as well," he decided. "Ethnically, Singh looks like a cousin, however remote culturally, but that will help and you sound more like them than I do."

Harinder nodded and Phil cut the channel.

Four years planning, and the wheels were finally starting to turn.

CHAPTER FIFTEEN

ADCON CRUISER ARANYANI

Kaur watched through the viewport as her shuttle returned, bearing the visitors. She hadn't been sure at first that the strangers would allow her shuttle to board, but they had a docking airlock that had been designed with all manner of options, so it had come alongside and carried the First Centurion and his staff.

The pilot had reported the arrival of Kosnett and his burly aide that had brought the drinks to Patte's reception, plus two females that had two and three stripes respectively, in addition to a small combat team they had been warned to expect. Senior Centurion and Command Centurion, using the odd structure *Aquitaine* had. Roughly the equivalent of Sub-Commander and Commander, if she was reading them right.

At least Kosnett had a number of females in senior positions. The *Gloran Empire* and the *Ewin Principalities* were almost completely male dominated. The *Dalou Hegemony* was nearly as bad. Only the pirates and the *Aditi Consensus* seemed to split things down the middle.

Kaur wasn't sure what that said about the two.

Namrata Nagarkar was in charge on the bridge right now as Senior Officer, since Kaur had Arya Chaudhari with her. Jagadish

Misra would stand out a little, being the only other male as part of this ceremony, but Kaur had wanted to make sure that Kosnett didn't think they were ancient Amazons or something.

The shuttle landed and engaged magnets with a thump she felt through her toes as the outer doors closed and the room began to fill with air.

This was not a formal, state visit sort of thing, at Kosnett's insistence. Two senior officers having a quiet tour of her ship, with Kaur's staff already planning her visit to the monstrous *Urumchi* in a few days.

Low-key diplomacy, which was the type she preferred. Especially given that Governor Patte only seemed to speak in exclamation points. There wasn't even a red carpet or a band, although her small legal affairs staff had needed to be yelled at a few times before they finally gave up that dream.

The inner hatch opened now and Kaur led the other two out into the bay as the shuttle opened up for Kosnett and his staff.

They weren't in formal lines, either side, but also weren't mingling.

Kaur studied the two new women as Kosnett introduced them.

"Commander Singh, this is Command Centurion Harinder Abbatelli, my flag centurion in charge of squadron communications," he said, gesturing to a small woman dark enough to be one of Kaur's cousins, although not African like the Fleet Ambassador had been.

Still, it was a good sign that he had many women around him. *Ewin* and especially *Gloran* could be taxing with their chauvinism.

Kaur nodded to the woman.

"And this is Senior Centurion Iveta Beridze, first officer aboard *Urumchi*," Kosnett said.

Kaur thought this one might be that north Asian that was occasionally called Mongolian or Siberian, depending. Several centimeters shorter than Kaur, with a heart-shaped face that was a bit plain, but the woman had a fire in her eyes.

"First Officer Beridze, this is my First Officer, Sub-Commander Arya Chaudhari," Kaur said now, indicating the woman.

Arya was taller, just a shade shorter than Kaur, but Kosnett towered over everyone here, including the burly male aide.

"And this is my principal Helm, Officer Jagadish Misra," Kaur continued, indicating the only other male.

Misra was only a little taller than Kaur, but he was average for most males. The aide was taller, but Jagadish was slim almost to the point of slender, so the aide probably outweighed him by twenty kilograms.

"My friends, we have several stations available for a quick tour, but given time constraints, we will not get to them all and my chef has a working dinner planned for everyone in three hours," Kaur said. "Did you have something in particular you wished to see?"

The first officer flinched but remained silent. Still, Kaur turned to her with an inquisitive face.

Beridze turned to Kosnett and got his nod before speaking. Kaur made a note of it. He had an extremely sharp staff used to taking the lead, while still stopping to ask the boss. Good to know.

"We watched many of the other ships split into two pieces to travel to the surface," the woman said. "*Aranyani* did not, but we were still interested in why and how you did it. None of our vessels are so designed."

"We suspected that," Kaur replied. "There were no obvious seams or lines along which to split *Urumchi*, but your ships are much more streamlined overall, compared to ours. We find it useful for hauling cargo to and from planetary surfaces, so our rear sections will remain in orbit, with most of the engines and JumpSails. Do you haul all cargo in such little craft?"

It was instructive that she turned to Kosnett rather than answer immediately.

"We have a team of what are called Fast Clippers," Kosnett said. "Dedicated cargo carriers that run between our home base and the staging area we set up outside the cluster. Those carry standard shipping containers in stacks down both sides, and also land on planets."

"Interesting," Kaur said. "Will they join us here at some point?"

"They will, but right now they are hauling our resupply," Kosnett nodded. "We'll send *RAN Viking* to update them in a bit, and eventually route them here on shorter runs."

"Isn't that a long logistics train?" Jagadish asked, almost biting his lips with nervousness at his possible effrontery.

"It is, but we had no way of knowing what we might find in the cluster," Kosnett replied. "We knew people lived here, but they might have been violently isolationist, or militant expansionists. Safer to approach slowly and introduce ourselves."

"Is that why you brought survey warships?" Arya asked now.

"Come," Kaur interrupted before things got out of hand. "We can tour the docking ring now and continue talking, but time is flying while we stand here."

She decided to lead, allowing her own combat team, who had been hovering as invisibly as possible, to form up ahead and behind, outside Kosnett's four and with her at the head of a column that allowed Misra and Chaudhari to mingle with the others.

She had seen the scans of *Urumchi* and *Viking*. If those were ships Kosnett considered peaceful explorers, she knew a great concern about what true warships would look like.

One only had to scan those seven escorts buzzing around like her own Moat ships might if she had to form a phalanx, to know that *Aquitaine* could be dangerous.

But they were all here to make friends.

She hoped.

CHAPTER SIXTEEN

Harinder had been trained by Enej Zivkovic as one of his first students when he ceased being Jessica Keller's left hand, so she was used to standing around combat commanders with egos and didn't let it bother her one bit. *First Expeditionary Fleet* would have failed many times but for a flag centurion exceptional enough that the Academy opened a new training program specifically because they finally recognized the need for such officers.

Like her.

Aranyani was a warship. Harinder had served on those. Flown them. Fired the big guns, even, before turning to a staff position more likely to let her keep her career going when so many of those combat commanders and their egos were forced into retirement by the shrinking fleet numbers.

Still, Kaur Singh reminded Harinder of Phil and Heather in many ways. Harinder had mostly trailed the others as they walked, listening to tone and accent as they toured the ship and saw the different ways that the *Aditi Consensus* built warships.

The tour had been a success, as Harinder would rate it. Beridze and Chaudhari had nerded out, dragging Misra into technical conversations while Phil and Singh had supervised.

Everyone had mostly ignored her, allowing Harinder to observe the *Aditi* people, as well as strangers in corridors or engineering spaces.

They were at dinner now, Phil and Commander Singh at the ends of a short, narrow table with her facing Chaudhari and Misra across from Iveta. The food was a curry heavy on tomatoes, turmeric, and some spice she could not identify, with both vegan and meat options available.

"I have a question," Harinder spoke up as folks ate, her eyes down the table at Kaur Singh. "The vessel *Saluki*, which is still in orbit. Am I to understand that you had chased them here and fought a brief battle over possession of that freighter you later escorted to the edge of the gravity well?"

"That is correct," the Commander replied, putting down her utensils now and grabbing her glass of water. "We are technically outside of our jurisdiction as an *Aditi* warship, but the *Zen-Mekyo Syndicates* also tend to operate outside of the law of most systems. They attempted to flee when we arrived, so it was necessary to convince them to stay put. *Urumchi* arrived while we were still here, so many of those various pirates have chosen to remain present to see what happens next. *Saluki* will not depart until we do, under the terms of their ransom, but we rescued our Ambassador, Trulan, who I have taken the liberty to assign to *Vilahana* while I wait for official orders."

"What will happen when you leave?" Harinder asked, confused on this point.

But she supposed it might be something like an *Aquitaine* cruiser sailing into a *Salonnian* port chasing after a *Corynthe* mothership, weird as that combination event might be. The Command Centurion would have been within their rights to claim *Saluki* and impress it into *RAN* service with a prize crew in such an outcome, and then claim a share of the prize money when the Lords of the Fleet eventually sold it off to someone or handed it to a wrecker.

"They will revert to what they were doing before we came

along, with the stipulation that they would not be allowed to visit an *Aditi* world for one year," Singh said. "What would *Aquitaine* do?"

Harinder turned to Phil for an answer. He was in command, and had the most experience with piracy of anyone Harinder knew.

"In previous wars with our neighbors, we would have possibly impressed the vessel into service," Phil said.

Harinder watched the confusion play out on the *Aditi* faces.

"Service, First Centurion?" Singh asked.

"Correct," Phil nodded. "Removed most of the crew and replaced them with *Aquitaine* sailors. Fly a *Republic of Aquitaine* Navy transponder. Trade the captured crews safely home later, assuming none of them had warrants issued by any of our allies. But, as I said, we were engaged in an all-out war with two of our neighbors at the time, while our closest ally shared a long border with a group that literally preferred to call themselves a pirate kingdom."

"Interesting," Singh said. "But eminently unworkable, as the major nations of the cluster only claim about half of the many inhabited systems, with the others having little fealty or trading with anyone who comes, like *Vilahana*."

"So when we go deeper into the cluster, will piracy be a problem?" Harinder asked now, letting Phil slide out of admitting *why* he was so famous back home.

"One woman's pirate is another woman's freedom fighter," Singh said. "And a third's armed merchant. Forbidding people any trade with *Aditi* for a year will drive their costs up significantly and is generally a good enough deterrent. But yes, there will be a few bad apples."

"Is *Vilahana* a graveyard for old ships, or a chop shop?" Phil asked now.

Harinder thought that Iveta's eyes might pop out, but she smiled at the youngster. And she caught the slight gasps from the two across the table, barely audible but there.

Singh raised both hands, palms up and moved them like a balance shifting back and forth.

"I see," Phil said. "When in Rome, I suppose. If nothing else, I might be able to get a good deal on adding a few local ships to my squadron for wider exploration, if I was of a mind."

Harinder could hear the emotion buried deep, but she'd spent a long sail listening for such things.

Phil wasn't angry enough to chew nails, but the first pirate they encountered might be terminally surprised by *Urumchi's* response. Especially with *Ground Control* and Iveta in charge.

The entire Navy knew about Phil Kosnett and his piratical adventures behind lines against *Buran*. Harinder wondered if the various inhabitants of the old *Altai Sector* would eventually deify him, given the close timing between his raids and the death of their former god.

Weirder things had happened.

A chime interrupted any commentary.

"Commander, what is your status?" a woman's voice asked.

Harinder thought that it might be Senior Officer Nagarkar, who they had met briefly, but was in command right now.

"About to commence dessert," Singh said. "What just happened?"

"Somebody just dropped a wolfpack on the edge of the gravity well," Nagarkar said. "The *Aquitaine* squadron growled at them, so they shifted well off to one side, but they're the same *Syndicate* as *Saluki*. And closing rapidly in an assault formation."

"I see," Commander Singh replied, hardening visible as Harinder watched. She turned to Phil. "Normally, First Centurion, I would immediately put you on a shuttle back to your vessel, to get you safely out of what might be about to happen, but I have concerns that they might attack such a craft and I wouldn't want that on my conscience. Would it be acceptable to keep you as guests a bit longer? At least until we sort out our new friends?"

"Indeed," Phil said. "And Harinder here is normally in

charge of flag communications for my squadron. If she could chat with *Urumchi*, we might be able to convince the others to play nice."

"This is not your fight, Kosnett," Singh said.

"No, but I came in peace," Phil growled back. "They don't get to ruin that for me by throwing temper tantrums."

"Thank you," Commander Singh said, rising. "Namrata, bring the ship to alert and make sure we have three spare seats for our guests on the bridge."

"Right away," Nagarkar said.

Harinder rose, willing to forgo the keer she could smell.

The opportunity to be on an enemy bridge in combat was utterly priceless. Phil and Iveta would be concentrated on this thing Nagarkar had called a wolf-pack.

Harinder wanted to see how the *Aditi Consensus* worked.

CHAPTER SEVENTEEN

Heather suppressed the chuckle that wanted to come out of her mouth. Iveta would be so pissed if anything happened right now. But that had been the risk.

"All vessels, this is Heather Lau aboard *Urumchi*," she said over the shared comm. "I have the flag, so route communications through the bridge. Everyone, all ships, to battle stations."

She paused exactly one heartbeat.

"Okay, people, I'm also handling tactical today," Heather called after muting her microphone. "Sensors, give me tonnage comparisons."

Leyla was already face down on her screen, typing furiously in spite of everyone having been close to the end of a shift and getting ready for dinner.

"Three vessels," Leyla said. "Largest one is a little lighter than *Aranyani* and looks more fragile, for lack of a better term. The other two are heavy frigates or light destroyers."

"*Aranyani* stand a chance?" Heather asked as everyone kept piling into seats and buckling themselves in.

"They don't think so, the way they are maneuvering right now," Leyla said. "And there we go. *Saluki* just broke formation with the others and is shifting to flank *Aranyani* as well. Singh and Phil are about to be hit on four sides."

"Squadron, prepare to intervene on the side of *Aranyani*," Heather said. "*CB-502*, *CG-504*, and *CG-505* shift forward now and take up escort positions around *Aranyani*. Defensive fire only until Phil or I say otherwise."

She cut the line again.

"Leyla, get me *Aranyani* on the tightest link possible," Heather said. "I need to know what Phil needs and they need to know they have help here."

She missed *Jellicoe* right now, and all those terrible primaries, but *Urumchi* would do. Her only complaint was that *Viking* was out of system right now, mapping the approaches to *Vilahana*. Another pair of Type-4s would really tip the balance.

"This is Sub-Commander Nagarkar, aboard *Aranyani*," a voice came over the line.

"Heather Lau, in command of the *Aquitaine* squadron while the First Centurion is aboard your vessel, Sub-Commander," Heather replied. "I am sending three of my corvettes down to provide you close escort while our friends decide how badly they want to start something."

Long pause. Probably muted and talking to someone at her end.

"Commander Lau, this is Commander Singh," a voice she recognized came over the line. "I have Kosnett with me, as well as the others. Stand by."

"Heather, this is Phil," he said. "The first password is BrightOak. What's the situation?"

"*502*, *504*, and *505* riding cavalry," Heather said. "I have a high flank and you've got *Saluki* looking like they're about to turn and fire into your ass."

"We noted that," Phil said. "Iveta is cursing up a storm right now, but we're safe for now and aboard an allied vessel for your rules of engagement. I'd like to defuse this. That may not be possible, but these people really don't think like Kigali or d'Maine, so expect someone to turn into Robbie Aeliaes after a few jousting passes."

"Roger that," Heather replied.

Robbie? That would be the *civilized* outcome.

Those folks only got civilized if they acted civilized right now. If anything happened to Phil and the other two, Heather planned to carve all three ships into small pieces that she could add to one of the junk yards floating around her.

"Engineering, stand by to bring all reactors and generators to maximum," she said aloud. "Gunner, lock on their flagship and stand by."

CHAPTER EIGHTEEN

Phil felt like he was almost back on the bridge of *Cyrus* again. Crowded, a little underlit, and with everyone facing either the outer ring of the room, or forward towards a big screen when they weren't looking at console screens.

Commander Singh had put him to one side, opposite the Sub-Commander, with Iveta on his right and Harinder on his left. Soft skin emergency suits were being put on by everyone as they stayed focused, but he didn't have anything to do, so his was already on with the helmet hooked to his hip.

Sharp crew, not excited by the possibility of impending combat. Maybe a little nervous at the odds, but they had relaxed when they realized that the three corvettes were friendly.

"*Saluki*, this is Kaur Singh," she said over a comm after Heather had dropped off. "I have your ransom. If you break it now, you will never trade at an *Aditi* port again, ship or crew. Stand down and return to your previous orbital position."

The hull thumped once and the lights flickered for just a moment.

"Titan bolts," Chaudhari called. "*Saluki* just put a pair into the shields on that side. Down seventy-three percent."

Phil heard Singh mutter what he presumed was a profanity under her breath.

"Keep the Shield Projector forward," she said after a moment. "Reinforce the nav shielding as much as you can and wiggle them around onto another facing as much as the situation will allow. I want all weapons on their flagship."

"Commander, if I may?" Phil said in a loud enough voice that she would hear him, but could ignore it.

Her eyes came around.

"I'm used to commanding fleets in combat," he said simply. "Harinder is my flag centurion. Put her on a comm to my ships and move yourself away from *Saluki* to let the corvettes get here to protect you faster."

"Can they take on *Saluki*?" she asked. It was a harsh tone, but not a sneer.

"They could probably take on the flagship by themselves, Commander," Phil replied. "I didn't bring a warship as my flag, so I brought escorts designed and refined by the last war. Let us help."

"This is not your war, Kosnett," she snapped.

"No, but I have a really big hammer, if they need it," he said. "Plus, I also have the ability to sanction them from all trade with *Aquitaine*, once other vessels come this direction later. They risk that, as well."

She paused and studied him for a long moment before nodding.

"Namrata, set them up with communications," she ordered.

"I have missile launch detected." Chaudhari voice overrode everything. "One of his consorts is an *Ewin* design. Strike that. Both of them are missile platforms."

"Kosnett, how good are your escorts?" Singh called nervously.

He looked at the main screen and noted why many of the faces in here had gone a little white. Phil smiled in spite of himself. Each of those ships had just launched ten missiles. *Saluki* had even put a pair out.

Probably enough to overwhelm *Aranyani* and do serious damage, forcing the ship to either withdraw immediately and flee, or be beaten into the same sort of surrender that they had inflicted on *Saluki* before.

"Your comm is open," Chaudhari said.

Phil felt his jaw jut out and his head come back. He'd never been there at that famous battle, but had been trained in the art by the man who had.

The Command Centurion who had subsequently taught everyone the art, and refused more than once to be promoted out of a Revenue Cutter because the old-style survey cruisers *didn't kill things.*

"*Aquitaine* squadron, this is Kosnett, aboard *Aranyani*. The password is Vigilance. I have the flag," he announced in a grim, angry voice. "All vessels, prepare to repeat *First Petron*. Repeat: *First Petron. Urumchi*, secondary guns only. Kill the upper wave of missiles. *Task Force 502*, the lower missiles are yours and then I want *Saluki* broken but not dead. They still have to answer to the Command Centurion here after the battle is done. All ships acknowledge and execute."

Phil wasn't surprised by the squawks of surprise emanating from the *Aditi* folks. Iveta was practically vibrating with suppressed energy while Harinder laughed once nearly silently.

Singh was watching the screen, so he got to watch her eyes get a little big as it happened.

Once upon a time—*didn't all the best stories start that way*— then-Yeoman Moirrey Kermode, not yet Centurion Lady *zu* Kermode because that came much later, had been tasked by Jessica Keller herself to become an Advanced Weapons Researcher. To commit *Mischief.* She had invented the Type-1-Pulse that the old *400*-series corvettes had had in their forward and aft weapon mounts, before Bedrov and a semi-famous Fleet

Centurion named Kosnett had suggested improvements. The *500*-series as it were, usually nicknamed the *Scorpion*-class.

The Guardians with him today all had a single Type-3-Pulse forward, again the invention of *zu* Kermode and that damnable pirate Bedrov, who had both been there at *First Petron*. But the Type-3-Pulse had proven most useful at *Second Petron*.

In between those two epic battles that seemed to bracket the modern generation of the *Republic of Aquitaine*, then-Fleet Centurion Arott Whughy had invented the Pulse-Two. The *Fribourg Empire* had been big on Type-2 beams in the old days, using them both offensively and defensively as needed, in an era of strike fighters and missiles.

But Bedrov had redesigned the Survey Dreadnought once he understood the implications of the new weapon. The *Strike Fighter Era* was over, back home. Missiles were rare to the point that *Urumchi* and *Viking* only had two tubes each, and those were mostly to launch special long-range explorer missiles to supplement short-range probes. Each ship only carried ten missiles total in their cargo bays.

Instead, *Urumchi* had Pulse-Two emplacements. Twelve of them. Three each on the corners, so nine Pulse-Two guns could fire right now when *Urumchi* shifted her tail around enough to bring the rear arc to bear in a furious broadside.

The wave of missiles detonated like it had run into an invisible wall in space. Twenty missiles, twenty-four shots if he'd counted it correctly. Still had power in the capacitors.

"And now *Saluki*," Phil noted calmly in the deadly silence of the bridge, like he was an announcer at a sporting event.

All seven of his corvettes had a Pulse-Two in the rear mount, the reason the class was called *Scorpion*, for that rapid chittering of deadly fire in combat. The ships were distinguished by the forward weapons array.

The two Guardians—*CG-504* and *CG-505*—had one Type-3-Pulse in the forward mount, instead of the Type-3-X the old boats had.

CB-502—Corvette/Battle—had **two** Type-3-Pulse on the bow. Four beams licked out, impacting a shield farther from *Saluki*'s hull than Phil would have imagined. *Aquitaine* shields were generally as close to the hull as you could get them, and the reason the hulls tended to be compact and streamlined. Smaller surface to protect meant more energy defending you.

Second salvo. Something happened to *Saluki*'s shields and one of the beams got through, impacting on a second set of shields. Second set?

"Shield Projector on *Saluki* is down," Chaudhari called, the only one in here making any noise.

Shield Projector?

Phil glanced at both women with him and got nods back. There would be interesting technology questions later, but first he needed to teach some people manners.

If he had to use a sledge hammer to do it, that would just be too bad for them.

Third salvo. Those inner shields weren't all that impressive. Somebody scored hull.

Fourth salvo. Metal began to sublime under the terrible impact of Type-3 beams on raw steel. *Saluki* started shedding pieces. Chunks large enough to be visible on telescopic optics.

"*Task Force 502*, kill his *Energiya* module," Phil announced with all the emotion of a customer asking the butcher for a particular cut of meat for dinner.

Fifth salvo. The reason the Type-3-Pulse was so deadly. You could just keep firing them as long as you weren't putting everything you had into engines or shields to try to flee.

Kigali and *CR-264* had been at *First Petron*. With nothing but Type-1 beams and a well-trained crew, he had utterly savaged multiple waves of missiles launched by Imperial ships and their piratical allies.

Only one friendly Mothership had been lost that day, and Phil had always wondered if that event had actually saved the galaxy from what was coming. Jessica Keller might have left the

RAN forever and retired to *Corynthe* had *Warlock* survived that *Götterdämmerung*.

"Second wave of missiles launched," Chaudhari called. "Line of target seems to be *Urumchi*."

"Namrata, arm long-range warheads on the titan bolts at their flagship and lock the Power Tap," Singh called now, broken out of her stasis by the ongoing battle.

Phil paid attention to the screen, knowing that his friends would also have things they learned.

Titan bolt. It reminded him of the secondary mode on the Bubble Gun as he watched it fire and impact, but it didn't implode and pinch. Just slammed into the enemy shields and detonated. Impressive, but not that impressive. Much smaller than bubbles.

"Power Tap locked," Nagarkar replied.

"Fire," Singh said simply.

That looked like a Type-3-Pulse, but Phil had just watched his impact on the Shield Projector thing that they used in the Balhee Cluster, so he could rate this new weapon. Perhaps twice as powerful. Four pulses a little faster than the Type-3s on a Scorpion, but then it was done.

"Flagship's shield is holding, but down fifty-five percent," Chaudhari called.

"Main Guns now," Singh called.

Phil watched those lash out. Yes, somewhere between a Type-3 and a Type-2. About where *Aquitaine* naval weaponry had been a century ago, before someone invented the Primary beam by desperately overloading a three and blowing it up in the process.

"Phil, this is Heather," he heard her come over the line in a laconic tone. "Somebody just fired missiles at me."

"I'm aware of that, *Urumchi*," Phil said. "Kill them and stand by."

Stand by. He wanted all eyes on *Urumchi* shortly.

Big, fucking hammer time was coming, but not quite yet.

The remaining four corvettes got into the act now, shredding the wave of missiles coming at them. Probably a little put out that Phil hadn't let them do that the first time, knowing the Command Centurions involved. People he had selected for that reason.

"*Saluki* is asking for terms," Chaudhari called. "They want us to stop shooting at them."

"Tough," Phil said, turning to the Sub-Commander with a hard smile. "Still, I can be benevolent. *Task Force 502*, one more salvo targeting his ass and any heavy weapon mounts you can identify. Then let him return to his earlier orbit. If he runs, annihilate him."

Quiet cries of outrage, but not from Singh. She was just watching him, like one might watch a butcher at work. Or a blacksmith.

Big hammer. Hot iron. The act of forging.

Random strangers do not get to show up and just open fire.

At least not without *consequences*.

Task Force 502 had been paying attention to the scans Heather had ordered. *Saluki* got thrashed as he watched, but this set of strikes were utterly surgical. And those three ships stopped short of unloading the full arc of their capacitors into him when the ship started to roll and yaw.

Looked like they had just lost their gyros. And maybe engines, from the way plasma was streaming out of their ass end like smoke.

"Put me on an open frequency for everyone in the system to hear," Phil said to both Chaudhari and Singh now.

The Sub-Commander nodded.

"Enemy flagship, this is First Centurion Philip S. Kosnett of the *Republic of Aquitaine* Navy," he began in a much louder voice. "This is the only time I am going to ask you politely. You will stand down and withdraw from combat. We will let this all be a terrible misunderstanding if you do. Otherwise, I will declare war on your Syndicate and destroy it. All of it, anywhere in the galaxy. *Am I clear?"*

Language lessons over the last few days had helped, as his Hindi was much crisper, to the point he sounded like Kaur Singh now when he spoke. They would understand him.

One way or the other.

Phil turned to the Sub-Commander and made a signal for her to cut the line.

"Local only," she said.

"Commander Singh, my apologies for usurping your position and role," Phil said carefully. "Hopefully, we can all sit down and talk like adults now, everyone having had their say. *Saluki* was under ransom for behavior, so they got what they had coming, but nobody else has currently taken any significant damage. Those people will determine what happens next."

"Agreed," she said, watching him like a hawk still but a little less frantic about her situation.

In addition to being surrounded by pirates, the woman had just realized that the strangers she had welcomed onto her ship were significantly more dangerous than anyone had probably imagined yesterday.

And *Urumchi* hadn't done anything but kill missiles, so nobody would be expecting it later if Heather brought the big guns to bear.

At this range, the surprise was likely to be somewhat terminal.

"Wolfpack maneuvering," Chaudhari called sharply, focused on her own screens. "Squadron coming about to their starboard but not accelerating. *Saluki* is not answering hails. *Task Force 502* is maintaining a circular escort position?"

She said the last with a bit of surprise, like they weren't used to that sort of thing.

Phil turned to Singh and got her attention.

"Where do your escorts normally fly?" he asked simply.

She started to say something, stopped, and then continued,

"We fly in the Phalanx," Singh said. "Smallest vessels on the front line. Cruisers like *Aranyani* in the middle. Ships of the Line remain at the rear, where their many Power Taps can pound an enemy vessel to pieces from safety."

"I see," Phil said. "And *Saluki* hitting your flank is not a soft spot, but also not one where you normally have many offensive weapons mounted."

"How do you build?" Singh asked.

Like her, Phil wanted to skip answering, as that verged onto military intelligence, but if it came to that, she would need to know.

"We normally mount heavy beams with hemispheric arcs on both sides of the ship," he said carefully. "Both *Urumchi* and *Viking* follow that pattern. We will show you when I have a chance to reciprocate today's tour. Hopefully without the exciting bits at the end."

"Hopefully," she agreed.

"Signal from the enemy flagship," Chaudhari said. "Addressed to the First Centurion."

Phil turned to Singh and waited. It was her ship. Her bridge. He was the interloper here.

"Go ahead," she said with a thankful smile.

He turned to the Sub-Commander and she nodded.

"Kosnett, this is Commander Utkin, aboard the *Ingham Enforcer Tango*," a gruff, sour, male voice came over the line. "We accept your offer. My vessels will attend to *Saluki* and begin repairs."

"The line is dead, First Centurion," Chaudhari said after a moment, but Phil wasn't surprised.

The man was a pirate warlord, much like Phil had once been. Unlike the *RAN*, however, he probably felt like he needed to get the last word in, just to show everyone how tough he was.

Phil decided to let him. They had just gotten their bluff called and their asses kicked. No need to finish them off. Because in a few hours Heather would be scanning their ships with survey-quality sensors, and every ship in orbit would likely be manning their own sensor arrays to see what they might discover along the way if they'd been paying any attention the last few days.

"Commander Singh, it has been my great privilege to have joined you today. Thank you and your crew for a wonderful tour," Phil said, unbuckling now and rising so he could strip off the softsuit and leave it behind. "However, duty calls and I feel I should return to *Urumchi* before the Governor calls to complain about our behavior again."

That got a laugh from the officers around him, which was the intent. He'd seen what he needed about the *Aditi Consensus*, as well as the *Ingham Syndicate* of the *Zen-Mekyo*.

He was starting to plan what the next stage of his exploration mission would be.

Now he just had to figure out who else might choose to be friends.

Or not.

CHAPTER NINETEEN

Heather was down in Phil's office once the three got back from the other ship. Leyla Ekmekçi was with her as well as Fleet Ambassador Aliza and Galia Abbasi off *CC-501*.

"Okay," Heather replied. "I get that they have a secondary Shield Projector that they can rotate as they need. Is it something we should consider? Their other shielding is pretty weak, comparatively."

"Possibly," Phil replied. "I am not so Pollyanna as to expect that nobody is going to try combat with us again. And that design makes wolfpack tactics more effective, which is probably why they did it. What about the two heavy weapons *Aranyani* deployed?"

"The titan bolt is, as you suspected, a direct-fire plasma-armed torpedo similar in design to the Bubble Gun, but much weaker. Long-range warheads suggest maybe a standard and a short-range for extra damage," Leyla spoke up now. "The Power Tap is likely what the pirates would have gotten if they needed to upgun a Type-3-Pulse into something heavier."

"What's their coverage arc?" Iveta asked.

Heather suppressed a snort. Always in the mold of Keller.

But the next time combat happened, chances were that Iveta would have tactical, instead of letting Heather have it.

"From the placement, I'm guessing one hundred and twenty degrees each on the titan bolts, but walleyed, so you can only hit someone with all four when you are centerline on them," Leyla replied. "The Power Tap is centered, so they fight linear. I'm guessing speed is everything in an encounter between warships."

"Agreed," Heather noted. "The wolfpack is a sweep, like cavalry. But if all *Aditi Consensus* ships are built like that, you'd have to go for the wings fast whenever you could. A squadron could rotate with you faster than you could charge around them, but the scans suggest that their Phalanx would shred someone trying to drive through the formation. Sharks would have had a party, but nothing suggests Capriole drives."

"How did the corvettes do?" Phil asked, turning to Abbasi.

She shrugged.

"Not exactly a fair fight," she said. "*Saluki* might be too much for anybody but *502* to handle alone, but those missile destroyers would be farts in a whirlwind against us. *First Petron* or even *Second Petron*, all over again. Wouldn't be surprised if Utkin sends them home as soon as he can, to find someone with beams or titan bolts instead. I would."

"Noted," Phil said. "Glad we got a chance to really blood everyone without a serious threat, but from here on in, all ships except *Viking* travel in pairs or better. I'll talk to Barnaby and see if he wants one of the Guardians with him, or if he'll rely on being able to blind anyone coming after him. What's on everybody's birthday present list for the next time I talk to Commander Singh?"

Heather looked around the group. They'd thrashed out the after-action sequence, aware that the pirates had underestimated the *Aquitaine* force, something that would likely happen exactly once.

"What other tech do they use here that we need to be

prepared for?" Iveta spoke up in response to his question now, when nobody else did. "They called the missile destroyers a *Ewin* design, so we presume the *Ewin Principalities* are missile-centric as a naval culture?"

"That would be my impression," Harinder interjected. "Chaudhari did not seem surprised at the missile storm, except that it might have been sufficient to overwhelm *Aranyani*."

"Do we have any scans that stand out, having lit everyone up?" Fleet Ambassador Aliza asked now, but like many on this mission, she'd done time on a warship before specializing. "There are fifteen warships in orbit right now and we now know what titan bolts and Power Taps look like."

Heather turned to Leyla.

"That *Dalou* boat," she said.

Leyla nodded.

"*Dalou*?" Phil asked.

"There is a space dragon over in one corner that mostly keeps to himself," Heather said. "Light for a light cruiser or maybe a heavy destroyer hull, by size. Bow weapon scans different signature than the *Aditi* or *Ingham* ships. Wings as well. Ship answers nav hails but that's about it. Not even sure they sent a Command Centurion to the Governor's party, now that I think about it, but they were here."

"The *Dalou Hegemony* is supposedly feudalistic in nature," Harinder replied. "But the prefectures are only loosely loyal to the center, most of the time. Privateers preying on other houses almost as bad as the various *Zen-Mekyo Syndicates*, from what Chaudhari was saying."

"One woman's pirate is another woman's freedom fighter," Phil quoted.

"Exactly," Harinder nodded. "I suspect we need to ask questions about them, and maybe confirm our suspicions about the *Ewin*. Leyla, have you seen any vessels with *Yaumgan* transponders?"

Heather stopped and thought about it. No, but she hadn't been paying that close of attention.

"Negative," Leyla replied after an equal thought. "Supposedly a relatively closed society that trades some, but doesn't really welcome outsiders."

"We'll use trade as a wedge, when we get deeper in," Phil announced. "But without any threats. We have an in with *Aditi*. Possibly we have made some enemies of the *Ingham Syndicate*, but I can negotiate that later. *Dalou* and *Gloran* are still wild cards, and both are more or less between us and the *Aditi Consensus*. Thoughts?"

"Invite every single Command Centurion in the system to our event," Aliza spoke up. "And their first officers, since they don't do Tactical like we do. Same rules as the governor had, but more marines and an open bar instead of cash. We've got trade goods we can swap for local booze, plus the exotic stuff we're bringing from home. Same for food, since I'm sure the Governor would love to acquire trade goods certain to be rare for at least a year."

"How soon do we schedule?" Phil asked. "Kaur Singh expected more ships, both cargo and combat, to keep arriving, now that news of us has gotten out."

"We should have a prize for early players," Heather spoke up. "Let's do something as close to immediately as we can, so we can take Utkin's measure, and turn around and have the ball of the season in something like six weeks, so people can run home and maybe bring back clan chiefs and First Centurions."

"I promised Singh a return tour," Phil said.

"Good," Heather said. "Let's host her the day before and they can sleep aboard. That's something special you aren't about to offer to other pirates."

She liked the chuckle that went around the group. Technically, she and Phil were the only two pirates in the room, with Dunklin just outside and the other two aft in Medical.

But if Phil and the other two were right, the whole damned cluster might just be one sea of semi-legitimate piracy, with everyone needing competent legal staff to keep it all straight.

Good thing they'd brought her as an expert, then.

CHAPTER TWENTY

DATE OF THE REPUBLIC MARCH 11, 411 RAN
URUMCHI, VILAHANA ORBIT

Phil wasn't one of those officers that stayed in his suite all the time and ordered people to attend him. Too easy to get isolated from the true harmony of the ship.

Back on *CS-405*, he'd made it a point to rotate every single bridge-qualified officer and crewman through both the main and emergency bridge crews on a regular basis, so everyone got to know everyone else. Harder aboard *Urumchi*, but Heather had continued that training on her own boats, and used it here.

Helped forge a team much faster than any other method Phil had ever encountered.

So today, he was headed aft, Dunklin in tow because that was what the man did when he didn't have specific orders otherwise.

The woman he was off to see hadn't been his first choice for Chief Medical Officer, but only because he hadn't even known she was available to recruit. Didn't even belong to the *Republic of Aquitaine* Navy, although she was now a Republic citizen as a result of marrying one.

The hatch opened and the Nursing Centurion looked up. Then did a double-take.

"First Centurion?" he asked in surprise. "Is there a problem?"

"Negative," he said, smiling so the man could relax. "Here to see the Doc if she is available."

"She should be," the nurse replied. "If you'll wait a moment, I'll check."

Phil took a spot in an empty waiting room and watched Markus pull out his bookreader.

"You'll be joining us," Phil instructed the man. "In fact, why don't you go find her other half and drag him along?"

"On it," Markus bounced out of the chair and raced out of the room.

"First Centurion, she'll see you now," the nurse said from the hatchway.

Phil rose and approached.

"My aide and *Stunt Dude* will be back shortly," he said. "Could you send them in as well?"

"Yes, sir."

Phil found himself in Dr. Au's office quickly. She was standing and he got a hug when he entered, but Sam was like that. And not subject to military authority, as she liked to remind him occasionally. Sometimes by hugging.

They sat.

"So what brings the evil pirate warlord to my station?" she asked with a twinkle in her eyes.

"Markus is gathering up Trinidad right now," he replied. "I'd rather only explain it once."

One delicate eyebrow went up and she cocked her head just so to show her curiosity.

Phil thought back to the first time he had met Au Aqal Corven Sam, then Chief Medical Officer on a *Buran* medical vessel his pirates had captured and impressed into service as *RAN Forgotten Mercy*.

Many of the ship-side crew had chosen their loyalties to their deathless god, but the medical staff had all been raised with the Hippocratic Oath, however many millennia old it was at this point. That had been the basis for all things, once Phil's folks explained to the others what had happened to captured *Fribourg* officers and crew.

The Disappeared.

Stranded on an inhabitable planet and instructed to work or starve, under the watch of guards and wardens secure in their fortress kremlins.

"You've gone serious, Phil," she said.

"Seeing you always takes me back," he replied honestly.

She nodded. They'd talked about it more than once, both before she vanished into the fogs of war after the rescue and then when she showed up at his recruiting office one day a year ago with her new husband.

The hatch opened and the other two men entered.

Trinidad Mildon. The famous *Stunt Dude.* Short for a guy, but still a little taller than Sam Au. Starting to gray now and a little heavier than when he'd been Phil's Dragoon aboard *CS-405.* Retired as a Senior Centurion afterwards and disappeared from history, at least as far as all the records had noted.

Instead, he'd gone looking for Sam. And found her, however impossible those odds.

With their god dead, the *Holding* had functionally come apart, and the *Fribourg Empire* had sent squadrons over to keep piracy from taking over. Eventually, retired First Lord Nils Kasum had accepted a role as Imperial Senior Administrative Admiral of the Blue beyond the old frontier.

The newcomers got settled quickly and Phil took a moment to breathe.

"So obviously, you are up to no good, Phil," Sam said, glancing at both *Stunt Dude* and Markus, who had been there with them.

Add Heather and it would be a reunion of sorts.

"Alien cultures, Sam," Phil replied. "*Aquitaine* and *Fribourg* are not that different at the end of the day, and everyone understands those gaps. We're out now out where the Republic is a distant land less than one person in a hundred thousand here has actually visited."

"You're pretty good at understanding those sorts of things," Sam said. "What was it here that you were looking for?"

"We're going to host some senior officers from *Aranyani* overnight next week," he explained to them. "Then an event for the Governor and all the Command Centurions in the system the next day. Or captains, directors, or commanders. Whatever term they use. Sometime after that, maybe six weeks, we'll do it again, but with the expectation that it will be a bigger event because folks will have had time to get messages home, so Admirals and First Centurions, plus Senators or whatever it is they do."

"And where do I fit in with all this?" Sam asked.

Phil caught her glance at *Stunt Dude*, who had remained silent. But he did that a lot more these days. Bringing Trinidad along had been part of the negotiation for getting her, and one Phil had gladly allowed.

Another pirate who could think on his feet, as it were.

"So the *Aditi* folks will all be military," Phil said. "Probably their Commander and a couple of senior folks, leaving Sub-Commander Chaudhari behind to handle emergencies. I want to include the two of you in the formal dinner, as well as the tour. And then have you present during the big reception. I've come in here with a dreadnought and a significant war fleet, so we need to make the case for peace and friendship next. Aliza Babatunde and her Ambassadors will all be there, but those are also all military folks, rather than civilians, so they think like I do."

"And me?" she asked. That twinkle was back.

"Nobody has ever accused you of being a thick-headed military punk, Sam," Phil laughed. As did the other two. "Hard-headed, certainly. Maybe more stubborn than me."

"Maybe?" she teased.

"Maybe," he assured her. But it would be close, either way.

"You want me to talk about *Buran* and the *Holding of Man*," she said.

"Among other things," Phil explained. "Heather and I have talked about what it would have been like had the *Lord of Winter* arrived with his fleets at *Vilahana* one of these days. I doubt they have a Jessica Keller, or a Yan Bedrov currently in a position to have done anything."

"It would have been bad," Sam noted. "Rumor suggests we are a century or more ahead of them technologically. Is that true?"

Phil noted her use of *we* to mark herself one of them. And she was. But she had been raised in a creche and ordered to be a doctor by an immortal *Sentience*, once upon a time.

And then *Stunt Dude* came along.

"Probably closer to fifteen or twenty decades," Phil offered. "They haven't have the war to the death that *Aquitaine* and *Fribourg* did, all the while *Fribourg* was trying to resist *Buran*'s expansion. There is a tremendous amount of destructive innovation wrapped up in these hulls. The only thing I haven't seen is any kind of carrier or snubfighter, but I presume that since they can separate off their booms, *Buran*-style, that it never occurred to them. Or it never worked out."

"Are they all really pirates?" *Stunt Dude* asked now. "I spend a lot of time with your marines, either in the gym or teaching them various martial arts forms, and that's the scuttlebutt."

"The major players have a much looser approach to colonization," Phil replied. "And aren't at war so much as constantly raiding and probing each other. The *Aditi Consensus* might be strong enough to eventually conquer the others, but I expect everyone else would suddenly make common cause and fall on all frontiers if they did. End result is an even-more-complicated mess, but one without any sort of charismatic leader that could unify them."

"Are we enough of a threat to do it?" Markus spoke up now.

But he was here as one of equals, rather than Phil's personal aide, and everyone understood that.

The Pirates.

"That's what concerns me," Phil said. "I hate to be so crass as to suggest that we make nice with *Aditi* to spall them off from becoming the seed of a new imperial pearl, but there's something to that. Similarly, playing everyone off against each other might convince them that we're softening them up for eventual invasion."

"Phil, I have a question," Sam said, suddenly more reserved than she had been.

"Go ahead."

"I am an outsider in your lands, just as you were in mine, back before," she continued. "One of the things Trinidad has shown me in recent histories is the more-recent rise of a harsh militancy in the Republic that wasn't there two or three generations ago. He said it comes from Kasum purging the fleet. What do you think?"

"You mean when the First Lord got rid of most of the old *Noble Lords*, in favor of the *Fighting Lords*," Phil said. Both of them nodded. "I would tend to agree with your theory. The Noble Lords had more in common with *Fribourg* than the underclasses, while Keller and many of her folks were Scholarship Kids, identified young and offered access to the Academy, when the aristocrats of the Fifty Families had tended to dominate it."

"What happens with the old clans sidelined?" Sam asked now.

Phil shrugged and sucked on his teeth for a moment.

"I've informally been in communication with Denis Jež," he finally said. "Keller's right hand during the various wars that made her famous. He's retired now and serving as an advisor to Karl VIII. One of the terms he has used is *Imperial Aquitaine* to describe a possible future."

"Would that be bad?" Sam pressed. "*Fribourg* was by nature

a conservative place."

"It was and remains so, in spite of a woman emperor and her foreigner consort," Phil noted. "Jež was talking in the sense that the end of the ancient Roman Republic came when a series of charismatic leaders arose, each about a generation apart. Their various wars for supreme power broke the Republic and practically forced the rise of the Roman Empire."

"Oh?" *Stunt Dude* asked.

His eyes got a faraway look Phil had learned to indicate that the man was going to go read after this. Trinidad Mildon had been a mustang, commissioned directly as a Centurion from civilian, rather than going to the Academy first or rising through the ranks, as many of the qualified enlisted men and women did.

"Sulla first, followed by Julius Caesar, followed by Octavian," Phil said. "Near constant civil wars for fifty or more years, because the Republic had grown too rigid for everyone to get along anymore, so things had to change. Looking at it that way, it is entirely possible that Nils Kasum might either be compared to Sulla, in how he purged the Nobles from the command of the *RAN*, or perhaps he sets the stage for a Sulla. Jessica Keller might have claimed ultimate power, had she been a different woman."

"Cincinnatus," Markus said. "Given ultimate power and then went back to his farm when he was done."

"Indeed," Phil agreed. "The exception that pretty much proves the rule."

"So who is coming up who might break the Republic?" Sam asked.

"I doubt that Premier Kasum, the older brother of the old First Lord, fits the mold," Phil said. "He only took power because nobody else had clean hands. Petia Naoumov will retire as First Lord of the Fleet soon, and everyone expects Arott Whughy to assume that mantle. He is a good Roman, in the sense of a builder and engineer, as well as a combat commander, but I don't see him doing anything to destabilize the Republic."

"So we have time?" Sam asked.

"We're here to see who else was out there to talk to and trade with," Phil said. "Identify if they were any sort of threat to the Republic."

"What if they are no threat at all?" Sam asked. "And instead so weak that the Republic could roll entirely over them whenever it wanted?"

Phil paused. He'd had a lot of conversations on the topic, but never in the context of Jež and his *Imperial Aquitaine* warnings.

"It would take a generation for us to build up the force to really hold all this if they were of a mind," Phil said. "Forward bases. New squadrons well beyond the first generation of Bedrov ships, with those retired for new things. Possibly we would need to take *Vilahana* like Keller once did at *Thuringwell*."

He turned to Sam and the others.

"Thank you," he said, rising. "You've given me a lot to think about, and from an entirely different perspective. If Commander Singh or her people spark some thought, please don't hesitate to tell me. Similarly if you get buttonholed during the first big reception."

"Are we here to conquer them, Phil?" Sam asked.

"Pet never told me, if that was the case," he said with a sudden smile. "And if that is the case, then they should have told me not to let the locals know about our technology. Nothing can stand against this squadron on anything less than sheer numbers right now, but I'm sure somewhere, somebody is looking for their own Moirrey Kermode or Yan Bedrov, to see what they might do to prevent us from invading."

"What will you do?" *Stunt Dude* asked, still sitting.

"I'm not sure," Phil answered honestly. "As long as they don't cause me trouble, nothing at all, I think."

CHAPTER TWENTY-ONE

Kaur noted the size of the beast as her shuttle approached landing aboard *Urumchi*. Any of the Ships of the Line she escorted were larger, but none of them had even three-quarters as much engine power available, according to Arya's scans of the flagship. Kosnett had not appeared particularly concerned with their current technology as a threat to his squadron.

After scanning what they had done to *Saluki*, she could understand why. Even his Commander, the woman Heather Lau, had seemed insulted at the number missiles fired by *Ingham* ships, rather than frightened or angered.

Just how deadly could these strangers be, if they had chosen violence from day one?

She turned back to Namrata and Jagadish, smiling to put them at ease. Her combat teams had been paired down to three people, and unarmed because she felt like having them come as visitors, rather than threats. And could so order it.

Both of her officers were nervous, but they at least knew some of the people they would be meeting, so this could be the basis of future relationships.

"Namrata?" she asked, catching the shadow come across the woman's face.

Namrata Nagarkar was of average height, so half a head shorter than Kaur or Jagadish. She could have been a fashion model, had she been tall and slender, but ended up in fleet service instead.

"As Kosnett is of Euro-ethnicity, and *Aquitaine* consciously follows an ancient Roman model for their culture, I have been reading," she began. "The Romans inherited from the Hellenes. I keep coming back to the Siege of Ilium and how that ended."

"The Trojan Horse," Kaur nodded. "That is one of the reasons we are undertaking to learn more about these people, Nam. To see if we should perhaps warn the Directors at home to begin building more ships and trying to find out about their advanced technology."

"Does this make us spies?" Jagadish asked.

But he was young. Only an Officer, two years out of school, while Namrata was a Senior Officer. Both were sharp, or she would not have them with her today. Still, he needed seasoning.

"Only of a sort," Kaur replied. "And an obvious type, just as they were when we hosted them aboard *Aranyani*. Be polite and friendly, without asking too pointed of questions nor telling too much. If you are unsure, ask one of us."

"Yes, sir," he nodded, a touch grateful.

Young, but learning quickly. He would go far, if he was of a mind do so.

They landed.

Kaur marked that as a measure of their value, that Kosnett let her shuttle land in his bay, rather than merely dock alongside. She watched the outer hatch close and the room fill with air, followed quickly by an honor guard of Kosnett's combat teams in nice uniforms.

Iveta Beridze met them, along with several others, and escorted her party through the ship to a heavy hatch deep into the ship.

The space took her breath away when she passed through the airlock. This ship had a forest in the middle of it. She could smell many things growing, and even hear birds chirping and flying around.

They were in a clearing planted with grass, rather than metal decks.

Kaur almost wondered if she had somehow been transported instantly to the surface of some planet, but for the metal ribs overhead.

"Welcome," Kosnett said as he stepped away from a group of folks.

Kaur took his hand, still a little off-center at being surrounded by *trees*.

"This is the actual Commander of *Urumchi*, Command Centurion Heather Lau," Kosnett introduced a woman even taller than Kaur, which was impressive. Not as tall as Kosnett, but he was a tall man to begin with. Still impressive.

Quickly, she met many other officers, including the Master Gardener responsible for this *arboretum*. One man caused her to pause and break the thread.

"You said you were frequently called *Stunt Dude?*" Kaur asked, wondering if something had been mistranslated from one of the other galactic tongues.

"That's right," the man said.

He was shorter than Kaur, but taller than his spouse, the interestingly-named Au Aqal Corven Sam.

"Before I served in the Navy, I worked in entertainment as a stunt performer for vids," the man said. "Then I trained other actors in it. Along the way, I joined the *RAN* for a time, and then left later."

"So you are a civilian?" Namrata asked.

"Technically, yes," *Stunt Dude* replied. "My wife is the Chief Medical Officer aboard *Urumchi*, and I occasionally train the First Centurion's marines in close combat."

Sam Au caught Kaur's eye.

"And you are not from *Aquitaine*?" Kaur asked, a bit surprised.

"That is correct," the other woman replied now. "I was captured by Kosnett's forces during the last war, where I met Trinidad. After I returned home, Trinidad came looking, living many adventures he is generally unwilling to tell even me. When Phil was going the other direction to see what was there, I decided that I wanted to see, as well."

Kaur was rocked back on her heels a little by the revelation. She pressed and got more of the story of how the two lovers had met. And the surprise of her life that five of the people around her had all been pirates at one point. Considering Kosnett's expressed opinion, she tracked him down, leaving the others to continue circling around and chatting with folks.

Kosnett saw her coming and gestured one of his people to wander off, leaving them alone but for her bodyguard and Kosnett's aide, who had also been with him on his grand sail. Markus. Kaur took a drink of the juice in her glass and studied the man.

"So you used to be a pirate?" she asked.

Better to simply start there than to meander around the topic and just confuse things.

"Privateer is probably a closer term," he said with a ghost of a smile. "My ship had broken down deep behind enemy lines in the middle of a war, and we did a number of things in order to get home. Capturing Sam Au and her folks was part of it."

"And yet she chose to find you," Kaur noted, still a little surprised.

"I have a reputation at home," he said, indeed smiling now. "My most recent assignment before this, I taught Command Ethics at the *RAN* Academy for three years, as well as Advanced Piracy."

"And the Emperor of *Fribourg* is a friend as well," Kaur noted.

"Diplomacy is one of my strong points," he laughed.

"Fighting was what I thought would make me famous, but there weren't enough hulls for Command Centurions, so my mentor arranged for me to be aboard a scout corvette instead. Later, I had to face the Emperor's Consort, who was commanding a warfleet powerful enough to crush my little squadron like bugs. He also sent me a present before this trip."

"So Phil Kosnett is a man that people trust?" Kaur asked. "A warrior diplomat?"

"An explorer," he corrected her. "All the other things are just part of the job description."

"So are you here to conquer us, Kosnett?" Kaur decided to simply ask the man point blank, to see what he would say. Or how he would react.

"I am here to see who lives in the Balhee Cluster, Commander Singh," he replied. "To see if it is worth building trade stations this far out, because the one-way sail is long. Would it be worth it?"

"Would it?" she pressed.

"I think so," Kosnett said. "Rampant piracy offends me, privateers behind enemy lines notwithstanding, but that was an act of war in the middle of one. Your neighbors remind me of *Corynthe* in all their bad ways, raiding and robbing."

"Would *Aquitaine* do something about that?" Kaur asked, marveling at how open the man seemed to be. But then, she hadn't asked any military questions as yet, and diplomats could always shade things as they needed.

"Personally, I'd rather the *Aditi Consensus* got together with the *Dalou Hegemony* and the *Gloran Empire* and cracked down on them," he retorted. "In many ways, *Corynthe*, *Lincolnshire*, and *Salonnia*, though I don't mean that in a derisive manner. All three of those nations are well matched, but not particularly centrally governed."

"I see," she said.

Kaur noted the approach of Heather Lau and smiled to include the woman in the conversation when she might have stepped away. Nam and Jagadish were both in small clusters of folks, apparently chatting amiably.

"Commander," Lau said as she stepped close.

"Command Centurion," Kaur replied.

"Having seen the arboretum, I wondered if perhaps you and your officers might be interested in touring some other parts of the ship now," Lau continued. "We don't do a boom separation like you do, nor the *Buran/Energiya* as our enemy did, but we can show other marvels."

Kaur turned to Lau and noted the same openness Kosnett seemed to be portraying. But then, this woman had been his Sub-Commander during his piracy, and also had a piratical nickname, just as *Stunt Dude* did.

"You were not afraid of *Tango* and the others when they fired missiles at you," Kaur stated.

"That's right," Lau replied.

"Why not?" Kaur asked.

If her bluntness was too much for them, at least she would know how to brief whichever director was sent when the folks at home heard about *Urumchi*.

"You saw our defensive firepower," Lau noted.

Kaur nodded.

"Those are based around what we call a Type-2 beam. The forward guns on the corvettes are based on a Type-3. Given your Main Guns as you fired them at *Tango*, our Threes are a bit more powerful and have a longer range than your Main Guns."

"Such did I surmise," Kaur said, mostly as a placeholder.

"*Urumchi* has Type-4 beams as heavy weapons," Lau said. "An order of magnitude more powerful than the Threes and normally something mounted on battlestations, rather than warships."

Order of Magnitude?

Kaur felt the room swirl around her, but only in her head and just for an instant. Could anything stand against them?

She turned to Kosnett and got his nod.

"And *Urumchi* is a survey vessel?" Kaur asked, unable to help her voice cracking in the middle.

"It is a dreadnought, Commander," Lau said. "One of our most dangerous weapon systems was removed from the design, freeing up space for the arboretum as well as cabins for all the ambassadors we're carrying. Plus, we only have two Type-4s instead of the four that dedicated warships like *Kongō* might. Kosnett came in peace. My job as his Command Centurion is to make sure that everyone else behaves as well."

Kaur nodded, still a little hollow.

"Yes," she said finally in a quiet voice. "I think I would like to see more of your ship."

CHAPTER TWENTY-TWO

Nam was doing the math in her head when Kaur sat next to her. They had been put in a suite for visiting ambassadors, with four rooms off a central space with a kitchen if they needed it, but Nam really just wanted to be away from people for a bit.

Kaur's face promised more conversation before the big dinner coming in about an hour.

"You were exceptionally quiet, there towards the end of the tour," Kaur noted.

Nam shrugged, then decided to share her deepest fears with her Commander.

"Not taking into account their lack of a Shield Projector, I'm not sure a Ship of the Line could stand in battle against *Urumchi*, Kaur," Nam said. "Their Type-3 was better than our Main Guns before they learned to pulse them. Our Point Guns are apparently comparable to what they called a Type-1, but they don't even bother to put them on their ships any more. Until both Kosnett and Lau mentioned how similar *Aranyani* was to their previous commands, the cruiser *Cyrus* and the battlecruiser *Jellicoe*, I was certain that the only thing protecting the *Aditi*

Consensus was *Aquitaine's* inertia of never having gotten around to us."

"And now?" Kaur asked.

"Now, we need to convince someone on *Aditi* to build new ships," Nam replied. "Maybe send someone to meet this Bedrov fellow and buy designs from Bedrov and Keller, so we can at least stay close as they continue to leap forward. We've been inside our little world for too long and the rest of the galaxy is leaving us behind."

"That bad?" Kaur asked.

But she was a Commander.

Namrata was only a Senior Officer, but responsible for the guns and the fighting. *Tango* and his wolfpack would have savaged them, in spite of everything Nam would have done to stop them.

"The entire future history of the cluster changed when *Urumchi* dropped out of jump, Kaur," Nam finally said. "We need to do something, and do it now."

"What about our neighbors?" Kaur asked.

"The *Gloran Empire* will steal or mimic anything they can lay their hands on," Nam laughed harshly. "That's why they frequently buy hulls from *Dalou. Ewin* is doomed unless they change their entire culture quickly. *Dalou* is probably making plans right now to sail across the gulf to *Aquitaine* to find out more. We must do the same."

"I need you here, or I'd send you in whatever ship I could scavenge from spare parts in orbit nearby," Kaur laughed. "Kosnett has threatened to do the same, and I have the impression that he could crew them, given the fleet at his command."

"He needs to be warned about *Zen-Mekyo* and *Dalou*," Nam said, meaning Kosnett and his people.

It wasn't her place, but she knew that Kaur had been hesitant.

"Most of what I might tell them are rumors, Nam," the

Commander replied. "Nothing anyone could prove without actually finding written documents."

"Would rumors be sufficient?" Nam asked. "Everybody knows that *Dalou* are secretly behind a lot of things, but always with plausible deniability. Privateers from some Prefect who mistook someone for an enemy of theirs. There are far too many *Zen-Mekyo* and *Gloran* ships that came out of *Dalou* yards. If they aren't building up the pirates as their own fleets, what are they doing with all the money they've gotten?"

She watched Kaur's eyes. Saw the way her brow furrowed.

"These are things for Directors and politicians, Nam," she finally said. "As a mere Commander, I am already skirting the edges of what might get me in trouble when all this comes out. At least until help arrives."

"*Tango* is alone with *Saluki*," Nam said, playing one of her trump cards. "That means Utkin sent *Algiers* and *Ironwolf* home, presumably for something with firebirds and who-knows-what other weapons. Something that *Urumchi* and her squadron can't just annihilate with the wave of a hand. They'll be back."

"And I have warned Kosnett and Lau of that," Kaur said, turning serious now. "You speak with Iveta Beridze as much as you can and learn how they will fight, when that time comes."

"When?" Nam asked.

"Kosnett threatened to *end* the *Ingham Syndicate*, Nam," Kaur said. "They will not take that threat lightly. If nothing else, having to bare his neck to the outsiders will cause Utkin to champ at his bit going forward. We are far from *Aditi* while *Ingham*'s base is presumably somewhere closer."

"Should we ask Kosnett to send *Viking* looking for them?" Nam asked. "Set one group of pirates to find the other? If nothing else, it would help us, if the Directorate finally decided to send a full Phalanx after them."

"Let me ask those questions," Kaur said. "Only one of us needs to be cashiered in disgrace if the Directorate decides we handled this situation wrong."

"As you command," Nam said. "But maybe I could volunteer, if they did build spare *Aquitaine* vessels from local junk?"

"I will keep that request in mind," Kaur said. "Now, relax and have a pleasant dinner, okay?"

"I will," Nam said.

But she didn't think she'd be able to actually relax.

The visitors frightened Nam perhaps more than they did Kaur, because they were here, and about to upset centuries worth of Balhee civilization.

Who would be left when it was all done?

CHAPTER TWENTY-THREE

Unlike hosting the delightfully-professional Kaur Singh and her officers, Phil wasn't about to let the rest of those bozos land shuttles on his dreadnought. Or even fly close.

And he'd stationed marines to keep everyone out of Sergey's greenhouse without written orders from him or Aliza. This event was being held in the forward observatory, configured for ambassadorial receptions with a big meeting hall, numerous conference rooms, and an oversized kitchen, with most of the spare cabins nearby in case he'd been hosting a conference of some sort that required folks to stay overnight.

The nine administrative shuttles aft had been sufficient to go get everyone who was coming. Commander Basant Utkin of the *Ingham Syndicate* had actually shown up in the middle of the crowd, rather than making a fuss about coming in last. *Tango* had remained close to *Saluki*, with Utkin's engineers getting the ship as repaired as it could be without a major drydock.

Phil secretly wondered if they were going to sell it to a merchant here in *Vilahana* to be stripped, and were just waiting until *Aranyani* left. If so, they were in for a wait, as Kaur had assured him that she was present until she got orders from a Director, the *Aditi* equivalent of a Fleet Centurion, to depart.

Would *Tango* remain as well? Were they waiting for a so-called pirate fleet? Or maybe all the pirates ganging up?

He could see sending *Viking* off to find a base he might need to stomp on later, if *Ingham* gave him any reason to.

Phil noted Utkin across a small crowd, glass in one hand though no food. The kitchen had gone all out this afternoon, but Phil had eaten a big breakfast so he could go all day without.

Basant Utkin was a big man. Burly in the manner of Markus Dunklin. Perhaps a little heavier, in the manner of a man exercising less as he aged, while Markus took every chance he could to sneak off to a machine shop where he could putter.

Utkin had muscles. In that, he reminded Phil of Alber' d'Maine, who had been religious about lifting heavy iron. Alternatively, perhaps one of the *Corynthe* pirate captains he had known, leftover from when rank was frequently a factor of personal duels with blades.

Nobody had mentioned that facet of Syndicate culture. Phil also hadn't dug too deeply.

Yet, he amended himself.

Aranyani had been present when *Urumchi* arrived because they had been chasing pirates to get their ship and their ambassador back. And *Saluki* had paid a heavy price for misbehavior.

Utkin noted Phil's look and broke away from the group he had been chatting with, walking this way with a heavy stride.

Phil practically smelled his marines come up an entire alert level, but the one in front of him was smaller than Sam Au. He wondered if aikido or jiujitsu were still practiced in the cluster. That might be an interesting surprise. Phil wondered if the Centurion in charge of the bodyguards had planned something like that. Or Dragoon Opeyemi. She might have said something.

Commander Utkin smelled it, too. He stopped half a pace farther away than he might have, like a bear sniffing out a trap, noting the small woman off to one side smiling up at him.

"First Centurion Kosnett," Utkin said, choosing to go ahead

and ignore the bodyguards for now. He bowed his head. "I wanted to thank you for understanding my initial confusion when I arrived in-system."

Phil tilted his head to nod back.

"We are strangers here, Commander," Phil replied ambiguously. "Much was in confusion, and I felt that perhaps if everyone could gather like this and chat, we might sort it all out without resorting to less diplomatic means."

"Are you really intending to bring the entire galactic arm to our neighborhood?" the man asked in a voice verging on sour.

"It is doubtful that they would all wish to come, Commander Utkin," Phil replied. "But I will file my report with the *Aquitaine* Senate before sending a long letter to the *Emperor of Fribourg*. She is an old sailing comrade from the wars, you know."

Phil figured he should just go ahead and let these folks know that they were swimming in a bigger pond now. He doubted that Casey *zu* Weigand would do anything to avenge him, but he could see an imperial exploration fleet being chartered in the next year or three. The sail was even longer from *St. Legier*, as they had a long border that just faced more or less across the darkness to the next galactic arm.

Eventually, someone would sail as far as the ruins of *Lost Earth*, though that wasn't on Phil's writ this time.

"So you are just here as a diplomat, as I understand it?" Utkin said, slipping that last half-step forward now so he could speak in a quieter voice.

"That is correct, Commander," Phil replied. "Without knowing how many inhabited worlds or nations we might encounter, I brought more than two dozen trained and accredited ambassadors that I might leave on various world to facilitate communications. However, nobody has really been able to explain the Syndicate structure to me. Do you have a homeworld?"

Low blow, asking a pirate where his main base was, but Phil

figured that they may as well just get it all out on the table now, however much Aliza might have chosen to kick him under a conference table were this a bit more formal.

Utkin recoiled a shade. Probably expecting diplomacy of the board room, rather than *by other means*.

"We have corporate offices," Utkin replied carefully, obviously hewing to the lie that they were all armed merchants who occasionally suffered *complicated misunderstandings*.

Phil wasn't fooled.

"Excellent," he noted. "Then perhaps we will be able to introduce an *Aquitaine* ambassador to your board of directors in the near future."

The man also wasn't expecting a naval officer who understood business. That much was clear.

Again, Phil had a three-year head start on most of these people in planning.

"What is your game, Kosnett?" Utkin asked, finally unveiling the image of a man who was a Command Centurion of Pirates, from the dark gleam in his eyes. Maybe a Fleet Centurion, even.

"Exploration," Phil replied. It was even honest. "You folks are too far away for any sort of serious commerce, at least this generation. I could see four or seven of the systems between *Vilahana* and the border ramping up trans-shipping facilities for more trade, but most of them are generally focused east instead of west, so they hardly know you are here, either."

"And you are not bringing war fleets?" Utkin practically sneered.

"Did I need them?" Phil countered. "Are folks in the Balhee Cluster likely to shoot first and only ask questions later?"

Utkin grew guarded. He'd done exactly that, and had perhaps suddenly remembered what had happened as a result.

And he was standing on Phil's Survey Dreadnought right now, surrounded by Phil's marines.

"No, First Centurion," Utkin replied carefully. "As you noted, a terrible misunderstanding when we first arrived, having only known that an *Aditi* warship had attacked one of our pickets, far outside their jurisdiction."

"I suspect that we are all a little outside of our jurisdictions right now, Commander." Phil smiled to take some of the sting out of his words. But his smile was still as sharp as a razor. "Hopefully, we can all come to a friendly settlement and get richer in trade than we might in other pursuits."

"I look forward to that, First Centurion," the man replied. He bowed again, perhaps a little more formally this time. "Until next time."

And he was gone.

Phil trusted that man about as far as he could drop kick him. At the same time, he didn't need to say that out loud. His marines had been of a similar opinion until he withdrew.

Looking around, the rest of the soirée seemed to be going well. Governor Patte was talking to the *Aditi* Ambassador Trulan, as well as Aliza Babatunde and Ikram Wattana, no doubt arranging for the latter's formal investiture as a local ambassador. Given the politics and geography, Wattana might end up being the second or third most important member of the whole diplomatic team, only behind the person eventually deposited on *Aditi* itself.

Heather was chatting with several people who all looked like merchant commanders, rather than warriors. Probably hoping for heavily-armed convoy escorts if Phil would allow it.

He wouldn't, but he could see making obvious his next destination and departure time, just to see who ended up close by and happened to be going the same way. Accidentally, you know.

One man stood out. Literally as well as figuratively, given that the other captains and commanders gave the man a wide berth, even in the relatively cozy confines of the reception.

Captain Makara Omarov, commander of the *Dalou Hegemony* vessel *Morninghawk*. Tall and broad in the shoulders, while extremely skinny. One hundred and ninety centimeters, but only ninety kilograms. He almost looked like a sail hanging limp in still air. At the same time, his black eyes didn't miss anything happening around him.

Phil decided to introduce himself less formally. Everyone had gone through a quick reception line at the beginning, but he had wanted folks mingling in safety, so they could just chat. That he had more of his people than all the visitors combined just meant that everyone had someone to talk to if they chose.

Omarov was standing aloof.

He picked Phil up, crossing through the crowd. It helped that both of them were at the high end for height, in a sea of folks shorter than Heather or Kaur Singh. Phil made a gesture for his marines to remain a bit back, so he emerged from the scrum and nodded to Omarov.

"Is the reception to your liking, Captain?" Phil asked the man.

Around him, he could almost feel the bubble of empty space grow another fifty percent. Were the others afraid of Omarov, or the *Dalou Hegemony*?

"It is quite interesting," Omarov replied in a deep voice.

Phil smiled and ignored the non-answer for what it was. Strangers perhaps ill-met in a bar during the kind of heavy storm that drove everyone indoors. Polite but not necessarily friendly.

"How would a *Dalou* Komyo hold a similar event?" Phil asked.

He liked the way the man's eyes snapped around and focused on him now.

Komyo, like *Daimyo* meant landholder, but *Dai*—Large— was reserved for the most important clans, while the smaller clans, like the one to which Omarov belonged, held the lesser title of *Ko*, or Small.

The man studied Phil for a long beat before speaking.

"It would be more ceremonial and smaller," he said simply. "A formal tea ceremony for the most honored three guests of the lord, followed by a meal. After that, important lords would retire to sake or brandy in a private room while their warriors remained on best behavior out front."

"Perhaps I shall be so honored, one of these days," Phil opined vaguely. "We are still learning your ways, the people of the cluster, so that we can interact without giving offense. My goal here was to allow captains and commanders to relax some and converse as equals. To ask us questions in an informal setting while I make the sorts of personal connections that determine my future sailing schedule."

"How long will you remain in the cluster, First Centurion?" Omarov asked.

"My writ runs at least a year," Phil replied. "However, I am also sending messages home regularly, so the Lords of the *Aquitaine* Fleet can modify that as they need. They had no greater understanding of what to expect than I did."

"Will you meddle?" Omarov asked, turning now so that his body was square to Phil where he had been a little off to one side before.

"That is not my plan," Phil retorted, leaving unsaid the general expectation that he already had, just by being here. "I hope to visit *Aditi* at some point. Similarly, *Ellariel* would be an important stop."

The capital world of the *Dalou Hegemony*.

"The Emperor and the Shogun would gladly welcome such visitors," Omarov said, lying with his mouth as his eyes told the truth.

Kaur Singh had referred to the *Dalou* as an insular people. Most of their colonies were tightly packed around a few central worlds, with a broad band of empty space outside that which formed a kind of neutral zone, planets largely off-limits to colonies from the others. At least without *Dalou* permission.

Lots of pirates tended to hide in that curve of stars, both

Syndicate as well as *Dalou* privateers, who might and might not be *ronin*, using the ancient term derived from the same cultural notes that seemed to drive the *Dalou*. It all depended on who one asked.

"What brings you to *Vilahana*, Captain?" Phil asked now, pivoting the conversation away from grand politics.

"Trade," the man replied simply. "The shipyards here are small and a bit primitive, as they mostly dismantle vessels rather than build them. Occasionally one finds a pearl amid all the dross."

"I had wondered," Phil observed, just to see how the man reacted. "Given those yards, I have considered building a few ships that could make regular mail runs for me, without having to tie up my warships. *Vilahana* looks like a good place to establish some sort of permanent base, given how it sits right at the mouth of the cluster, as seen from *Aquitaine* space."

The man's eyes flared, but he remained silent.

"Tell me," Phil continued. "Are there many other gaps that have been found, leading in and out of the cluster from other directions?"

There. A twitch. Not much, but something.

"None I am aware of," Omarov replied evenly after he got himself under control again.

He held up his glass now and noted the low level.

"It appears I am in need of a refill, First Centurion," he said, already starting to walk away. "You'll excuse me?"

"Of course," Phil replied quickly, before he was talking to the man's back.

So, there *were* other avenues. And a *Dalou* captain didn't want to discuss them with an outsider. Phil wondered if they led to any secret bases outside the cluster, or perhaps buried in the walls of the nebula itself and impossible to get to easily.

Or did someone have a back door he could take, slipping out of the cluster to sneak in around a curve and attack someone else from behind?

Phil made a note to talk to Barnaby and see if *Viking* might track such things down. Pirates required bases to operate from. Places to pick up supplies and recruits, as well as to perform maintenance and repairs. They would want quiet systems to do it. Those didn't have to be in the band of neutral stars around the *Dalou* core.

Or had *Urumchi* interrupted Captain Omarov as he was intending to meet with some Syndicate contact? In addition to *Ingham*, there were vessels from the *Hamath* and *Gilas* clans present, all pretending to be good, little merchants while Phil and Kaur Singh were around.

"What's so funny?" Heather asked as she stepped close.

"Wondering if our presence here, acting like an anchor to hold so many ships and people in place, is going to have a measurable impact on piracy in the sector this quarter," he replied with a chuckle.

"Nobody here is who they appear to be, with the possible exception of Kaur Singh."

"She is a Command Centurion facing a brutal and public court martial when she gets home, regardless of what she does here," Phil replied, turning to face the woman. "Whether they give her a medal or her walking papers is still outstanding."

"Do we care?" Heather asked quietly.

"We need allies," Phil noted. "I have no doubt we could cut a swath of destruction, had that been our mission, but even threatening them risks hardening everything into a marriage of convenience. I'd rather turn them into a whole series of trade partners and allies, since there is still the next galactic arm over to explore, one of these days."

"That will be my mission, after you retire, First Centurion," Heather laughed.

Phil joined her, but noted that she was probably right. His career would be capped nicely by whatever he did here, today. Allies or enemies would determine his own court martial in the court of public opinion back home.

However, he was off to a good start, looking around. Now, he just needed to start building positive momentum, even as he was surrounded by liars, rogues, and pirates.

Other pirates.

He might yet need to teach these folks a thing or two.

CHAPTER TWENTY-FOUR

Aliza Babatunde studied the man standing in front of her, wondering if he was going to actually stamp his foot angrily and get shrill at her, like a teacup Chihuahua her parents had owned when she was young. His face promised something like a fit brewing.

Aliza wasn't used to being tall, but partly that was being around Phil and Heather as much as she was. Governor Patte was short and compact for a male. A little pudgy, but enormous when it came to personality.

"Technically, that is not my decision to make, Governor Patte," she replied to the man, couching her words and tones into softness so as to not give the man any hard edges to bounce off of.

"Are you not the Fleet Ambassador?" he demanded tartly, still looking like a temper tantrum might be in the offing, although she doubted it would be anything more than show.

Governor Annen Patte had lost control of the narrative early on, and was desperate to remain relevant. Aliza didn't bother telling him again that *Vilahana* was likely to turn into a major port as a result of all this. The Teacup Chihuahua still felt the need to bark.

"I am *a* Fleet Ambassador, sir," Aliza agreed carefully, pointing at her arm. "But that is a rank in the *Republic of Aquitaine* Navy, Governor. You will note that I have four stripes. First Centurion Kosnett has five. That was intentional, on the part of our superiors, to make sure that everyone and everything fell under his plenipotentiary power. My Command Diplomatic Centurions have three stripes, and are the peers of Command Centurions Lau and Abbatelli, although we are not in the same chain of command."

"So Kosnett makes all decisions?" Patte snapped.

"The First Centurion has the authority to veto me, Governor," she smiled. "By design. However, I do not believe he is as firmly committed to certain things as you might think. Perhaps we should go chat with him and see if he is amenable to amendment."

She stepped close and took his arm like she was escorting him into an event. That seemed to mollify the man some, as he began to relax. Annen Patte was still the barely-competent governor of a fringe world, but he was playing a game to parlay that into something much larger. Or at least more profitable for the man, if she read him right.

He wasn't as open and readable as the morning newssheet, but almost, Aliza decided.

She located Phil and steered Patte in that direction. Heather was close by as they approached, and remained, but faded off a shade as she took the temperature of the players.

Nobody *ever* gave Heather Lau credit for just how dangerously competent that woman really was. Aliza knew better.

"First Centurion," Aliza said as they all got close. Using his title put Phil on notice that things needed to be more formal. As did holding Patte's arm like she was. "Governor Patte would like to inquire about the possibility of holding the coming conference on the surface of *Vilahana*, using part of his palace, rather than keeping it aboard *Urumchi*."

Phil had already gone official and distant, just watching the way she had approached. Now, he looked like some sort of Patriarch from one of the ancient religions. He studied her for cues before turning to Patte and giving the man a frosty smile.

"I see," Phil began in a stentorious tone. "As I understand the current political situation, Governor, while *Vilahana* does not belong to any of the major nations, happily trading with all comers, you might have previously been a bit more beholden to the *Zen-Mekyo Syndicates* in ways that others might not have considered entirely beneficial to the greater galactic society."

Aliza already knew from the way he was standing that Phil was going to play Bad Cop, so she was prepared to suppress the snort that wanted to express itself right now. At least she was expecting the jolt of indignance that shot through Patte.

Nobody likes being called a criminal to his face. Especially when it was the truth. Slander is only a problem when someone is lying, after all.

Patte got his emotions under control a little slower than Aliza was expecting, but he might have forgotten that she was holding his arm and could read him by touch, too.

"There is merit in your thoughts, First Centurion," he said, for once leaving off the exclamation points he liked to talk in. "We should look on this an opportunity to build a new future for the Balhee Cluster. One where trade with *Aquitaine* becomes a much greater thing."

"I had a similar thought, Governor," Phil said now, springing a trap on the man that Aliza saw coming a kilometer away. "We should work towards a treaty that establishes a permanent presence of *Aquitaine* ships at some future date, to help keep a lid on smuggling and petty crimes in the vicinity. That way we can maintain patrols outside the Cluster while based here, as we'll be expecting more trade to eventually lead to bases being built nearby by other interested players."

Aliza did not snort. Did not even breathe. She hadn't been expecting Phil to go so far as to demand an orbital fortress with *extraterritoriality.* However, the threat of other players coming along and maybe engaging in even worse piracy was a useful hammer. Patte had his fingers in all sorts of local shenanigans that outsiders wouldn't care about. They might even work to remove him if he got in the way of their own profit, or at least bribe the local merchants for a different governor.

Phil had just mousetrapped the man, and done it nicely.

Aliza winked at Phil with the eye Patte couldn't see. She now had the basis of a lovely negotiation that Wattana could work from. And a stick to go with the carrot.

Phil smiled as Aliza felt the shock pass through Governor Patte's arm.

"So in the interests of furthering trade, I can see the merit in having such a conference at your palace, Governor Patte," Phil continued a moment later. "It reminds everyone that you have chosen to put the old ways behind you and work towards a much more glorious future. What say you?"

Aliza felt the surge of anger. That moment of pure rage that the man carefully contained, boxed up, and stuffed in a footlocker, unwilling to let something so petty as his personal feelings stand in the way of possibly getting even richer than he already was.

Phil Kosnett and *Urumchi* were likely to tack at least one zero on the back of the man's net worth in the next decade.

Presuming he didn't give anyone a reason to have him killed in the meantime.

"Yes," Patte replied after a long moment. "I see the merits of your thoughts, First Centurion. I will need to consult my staff of course, but I look forward to working with Ambassador Wattana on making this the biggest thing that has ever happened to *Vilahana.*"

"Excellent," Phil said, glancing her way and smiling.

"Now, Governor Patte," Aliza said, turning the man to face her so Phil and Heather could slip away unseen. "Let's go find

Ikram Wattana and maybe start working out some of the details, while we have so many players handy that we might consult."

She guided him off, noting that the man was still a little in shock. It wouldn't be that bad. She'd only take advantage of him somewhat, knowing that Phil had set out a hard line threat that everyone would want to avoid.

It still gave her a lot of space to maneuver. And she'd still make sure that Annen Patte got rich in the process.

CHAPTER TWENTY-FIVE

Kaur had let everyone relax for a day after the event on *Urumchi*, just so they could decompress and organize their notes. Her own had run several chapters, once she started brain-dumping everything she had seen or thought of during the two days aboard the enemy flagship.

Enemy?

Perhaps, yet. Phil Kosnett was doing a masterful job of discombobulating everything and everyone, just by being here. Even more than *Aranyani* had done, chasing *Saluki* down to rescue an ambassador.

She knocked on Namrata's hatch now. As Weapons Officer, Nam would be the one who had paid the most attention to things Kaur needed to think about.

The woman opened her hatch a moment later and stepped back. It was late in the day and Jagadish was on the bridge in command right now, but everyone was probably still awake if Kaur needed them.

"Commander," Nam said, moving to her bunk and leaving the chair open.

Kaur sat and gestured Nam to do the same.

"We are off the record, Nam," Kaur said simply after she

closed the hatch. "I want your impressions of *Urumchi* as a warship, separate from Heather Lau's crew."

"If that is merely an undergunned Survey Dreadnought, as they claim, then an *Aquitaine* squadron could utterly shatter anything less than a full *Aditi* fleet that came at them," Nam replied, her voice growing a little hoarse with suppressed emotion. "Their Type-4 beam is bigger than anything we mount, even on any but the largest of our stations, Commander. The Type-3-Pulse is not quite the match of a Power Tap, but they have the generators to keep firing them as long as they want. And no missiles could reasonably hurt them, unless we dropped an entire minefield of weapons and triggered them from short range."

"I noted that they barely carry any missiles themselves," Kaur said. "Ten in total, with only two tubes."

"And all ten of those could have their warhead swapped out for a probe package, Commander," Nam said. "I was interested in Heather's questions about small fighter craft. Could you imagine one- or two-person attack shuttles? Perhaps armed with their own missiles? Why does nobody build them?"

"I don't know," Kaur said. "Perhaps because we can't build a JumpSail small enough? Those would only be useful at short range. Perhaps defensively, but we build minefields instead, both explosive and beam-armed. Cheaper. Easier."

"Agreed," Nam replied. "And probably irrelevant now, if we can obtain the secret of the Pulse-Two, or a license to manufacture our own."

"There are a great many things we need to get from Kosnett and his people," Kaur said. "Technology transfers appear to be going one-way, though."

"They do not use Shield Projectors," Nam reminded her. "Would that make them even deadlier? And I have not seen any indication of an Ion Gun, but those are usually pirate weapons, since it lets them capture ships without necessarily damaging them."

"As to the former, I cannot say," Kaur noted. "The latter might be useful if they chose to suppress us without inflicting massive casualties in the process."

She paused and reflected for a moment.

"Nam, your job right now is to do a rigorous survey of all the weapon systems and technology we do use, anywhere in the cluster, with an eye towards how that might balance the trade scales with *Aquitaine*," Kaur said.

"Should we include *Yaumgan*?" she asked, only slightly kidding.

"As their own appendix, perhaps," Kaur said. "They are even more insular than *Dalou*, and probably have all manner of ideas they have dreamed up and never bothered trading with anyone else. We're just barbarians, as far as they are concerned, after all."

Nam laughed.

"Still, could you imagine some of *Yaumgan*'s weirder ideas mixed with *Aquitaine*'s?" she asked. "The philosophers meet the engineers?"

"It would either be a match made in heaven or hell, Nam," Kaur chuckled. "Make that appendix a separate volume for now, and we'll approach Phil in a more relaxed situation to talk about giant fighting robots that fly through space."

"As you command," Nam giggled. "How quickly can we get him to *Aditi*?"

"Not anytime soon," Kaur let the frivolity flow out of the room. "We await whatever Director can make it in time for the conference on the surface. From there, I suspect that there are more interesting planets Kosnett might visit on his way inward. But mark this: Phil Kosnett will not have his head turned by pretty things or exotic ideas. That man and his crew are starkly professional in a manner that nobody here even begins to appreciate. We might be the closest, and none of us are anywhere near as bloodthirsty as the outsiders. They play a polite game, but not one of them would hesitate an instant to cut someone's throat if they thought it necessary."

She hadn't meant to make Nam gulp suddenly, but better the woman realize that now and prepare, than find out the hard way later.

Kosnett and his people were no fools. They were up to something.

Kaur Singh just needed to find out what.

CHAPTER TWENTY-SIX

Basant Utkin exited the shuttle and strode right past the supposed honor-guard of troops Commander Liefan had deployed there as an escort. They hurried in his wake, just barely keeping up as he stretched his legs.

He made his way to the bridge, scowling at anyone attempting to intercept him.

Someone must have said something, because Andrea was already standing when the hatch opened, one hand close to the pistol on her hip but not resting on it.

As if he would come all this way just to shoot the woman. *Tango* could have destroyed *Wulfa* and most of the rest of the ships in the system would have probably celebrated one fewer pirate in the galaxy.

"Your office," he snapped, turning and moving that way before anyone else did.

Rather than argue, she followed, moving past him when he sat and taking up her spot behind the desk.

"I can see that your manners haven't improved much," she said blithely, but only after the hatch was closed.

Basant had never formally married. Never found a woman worth pursuing. Andrea Liefan had come close, but had made it clear fifteen years ago that she wasn't any more interested in domesticity than he was.

And the two of them serving on one ship would never work. Oil and flames.

"Is it done?" Basant asked, striving to be at least a little polite.

Stepping off *Tango* always made him uneasy. Too many places with warrants out. Too many bounty hunters that might see their chance, if they happened to encounter him on the surface of a planet. Even *Vilahana* while *Aquitaine* and the locals were enforcing security regimens.

"It is," she replied without baiting him again.

Even Andrea understood that there were short limits to his humor.

"How soon until they notice?" Basant asked.

She shrugged, but that was probably the most honest answer anyone could give.

"The rock has been in a solar orbit with *Vilahana* for thousands of years," Andrea replied. "Crossing back and forth without ever touching. The hardest part was calculating the force necessary to get an impact on the day and facing you wanted. I still don't understand why you think we need to destroy *Vilahana*, nor why the Board of Directors was willing to go along with you. Plus all the mines that are slowly deploying themselves from the two containers we dropped on the surface of the moon."

"*Aquitaine* being here changes everything," Basant snapped. "Kosnett is a cop, plain and simple. They will push to clean up piracy in the cluster. Whether anyone else likes it or not, but we both know that the *Aditi Consensus* would turn cartwheels down the main corridor at the chance. *Gloran* suffers us because we can get them technology they don't have. *Dalou* is playing their own long game. Hell, even the *Ewin Principalities* would rather not exist in a universe where every ship had pulse technology to devastate their missile swarms."

"And destroying Patte and his world?" Andrea asked. "Because we're about to drop a rock nearly twenty kilometers across on them. If word of that ever gets out, our bounties get zeroes tacked on."

"Patte has changed sides, Andrea," Basant replied. "He's going to help Kosnett. Maybe let them build a major fleet base right here so they can help patrol inside as well as all the approaches. Whether they use that to conquer *Aditi* or ally with them, the outcome is the same. *Vilahana* stops being a trade port for us, and turns into a cork keeping us bottled up while they hunt the Syndicates down. When something happens, we're going to blame the invaders for destroying *Vilahana*. Maybe we kill the Governor. Maybe not. Kosnett will escape, unless something exceptional happens, but if everyone thinks they did it…"

He shrugged.

"Big risk," Andrea said. "Hopefully commensurate rewards. Certainly, a major roll of the dice by the bosses. But you didn't need to come all this way to hear the news. Why are you really here, Basant?"

He studied the woman. Saw the amazing woman who had first caught his eye twenty years ago. Average height but athletic and muscular, even today. Short brown hair shot through with polished steel. Deadly eyes.

"Are we secure in here?" he asked.

"It gets more dangerous than a discussion about blowing up one of our allies?" she asked, eyes opening wide for a moment before they hardened down into squints. "Bombarding an inhabited planet? What are you up to, Basant?"

"The Board isn't prepared for what's coming, Andrea," he replied. "They're going to go back to the old thinking when this is done. The Pressor Beam is new, but the idea of bombing someone who double-crossed us isn't. You just have the one ship currently configured to nudge an asteroid out of alignment when

I need a big hammer to drop on some little chiseling punk like Patte."

"You think we should shake up the board?" she asked, leaning back now to watch him.

"Take it over," he replied. "You and me. We've got allies we can convince to purge the softer elements. The ones who will try to cut deals with *Aditi* or *Dalou* for some sort of political cover. If *Aquitaine* gets a foot in the door here, we'll never push them out of the cluster again."

"And you trust me not to tell people about this conversation?" she asked him.

"You just pushed an asteroid into the path of a planet, Andrea," he reminded her harshly. "Just following orders won't save you if someone wants to swear out a death warrant for you and *Wulfa*. I might have asked the Board to sign off on it, but that just means all of our necks if someone talks. You and I could have been a thing, once upon a time, but that didn't work out then for reasons we both understood. Hasn't stopped the occasional weekend fling when we were both in the same port since. Now, we have to step up and stop *Aquitaine* and *Aditi* from conquering the whole cluster and mashing us under their cop feet. I'm not asking for your body. Just your soul."

She studied him for a long moment. Basant wasn't sure if she would take the offer or rethink a life of crime, but they were all looking at forever in an *Aditi* prison if they were ever caught at this point.

"I don't believe you," she said suddenly.

"Excuse me?" Basant asked, sitting up straight.

"About not wanting my body," she retorted with a smile. "If this is a conspiracy to take over the board and burn a lot of people, take me to bed and prove just how committed you are."

Occasionally, he had wondered if the woman verged on black widowhood, but he stood now and held out a hand.

He'd come here looking for an ally.

Maybe, he'd accidentally found a partner in crime.

FRYANY PORT

CHAPTER TWENTY-SEVEN

At least the locals had selected an excellent site for a city. Standing on the wide balcony of Patte's palace, Phil could see mountains not far away, stair-stepping up from hills as you moved east past the lake that formed the back side of Fryany Port, itself facing a sheltered harbor on the west and framed by open coastal plains both north and south.

Everything around here was green and growing. The moisture coming off the sea was forced to rise to get over those mountains so it fell as rain nearby, watering things in every season and keeping everything generally cool and paradicical. Beyond that range of glacier-capped mountains he could see, things were gold or brown, respectively as your got deeper inland.

He was looking roughly southeast, where an extinct volcano topped with a glacier dominated the distant skyline and the low sprawl of the port city itself spread out around him. Patte hadn't selected the location for his palace, having inherited it from numerous previous governors, but Phil got the impression that the man had turned it from a cold, bureaucratic place into a residence reminiscent of the ancient aristos of Earth, men and women who had used their inherited wealth to commission art, sculpture, and music that was still played today, however many millennia later.

And it was a little weird, being serenaded by a quartet playing wooden instruments by drawing polymer cords across metal strings. No amplification. Nothing recorded.

Ancient, but in a good way.

Footsteps announced company, but the three semi-invisible bodyguards around him at all times didn't say anything. Wasn't Markus, as he had a heavier tread when he walked.

Phil turned to see Kaur approach. She had a glass of something in one hand from the reception Phil had snuck out of. Still on the grounds, but down a couple of discreet hallways and up a flight of stairs.

"Stalking me?" Phil asked with a grin.

He had come to like Kaur Singh, both as a Commander and a person.

"You might be the reason we're all here, Phil," she retorted, moving to stand next to him and leaning against the railing. "Lovely view."

"That's why I hide here when Patte doesn't need me," Phil said.

"This is your party," Kaur said.

"This is Patte's party," Phil laughed. "The conference doesn't start until tomorrow, so we're just welcoming everyone from everywhere tonight with drinks and finger food as a way to play sop to the Governor's ego."

"He does stand to get rich," she pointed out. "More rich."

"We all do, if we can approach this like adults, Kaur," Phil said, joining her and staring at that cone of a mountain.

"Adults, Phil?"

"The Syndicates exist because too many people are trying to practice autarky," Phil replied. "Trade just with their own colonies and freeze everyone else out of captive markets. That breeds smugglers. Smugglers need things to trade, so that breeds piracy, however genteel and polite everyone pretends to deal with it. You hit *Saluki* the first time just hard enough to make your point, rescue your freighter, and hold them hostage here until you left."

"True, but that's always been official policy, Phil," she said, turning now to face him. "You won't be able to change that."

He smiled. It wasn't an especially friendly smile, but it also wasn't aimed at her.

"I disagree," he said simply. "The whole point of inviting everyone here was so that *Aquitaine* could start negotiating treaties and sending ambassadors off to various places without me having to sail everywhere. But more importantly, it lets all of you get together and have side conversations. That should bring trade. If the Syndicates were more interested in legitimate business, I'd be tempted to hire them to start hauling cargo to and from *Vilahana*, just to make it easier for everyone."

"And making Patte rich."

"And that, yes," he said.

"What if folks don't want to trade?" she asked, circling back to the old question they had hammered back and forth individually as well as in group visits.

"Then they risk being left behind," Phil smiled. "Nam Nagarkar wants Pulse Technology. I presume your Director will as well, since it alters the balance of power throughout the cluster. Everyone else will want it at that point, and then it becomes a need, in order to keep up."

"What does *Aquitaine* want in trade?" she asked.

She'd pressed him before, but at the end of the day Kaur Singh was just a Command Centurion, unable to negotiate treaties, working instead on the personal relationships that would help the *Aditi Consensus* long-term.

"Nam had a couple of things on her list that I found interesting. However, I'm not an engineer, Kaur," he replied.

"Shield Projectors are nifty, but we have heavier shields that use a different technology to begin with, and I'm not sure if we can marry the two without a lot of work. The Pressor Beam might be useful for mining and construction, though at present I can't see a military use. The *Dalou* firebirds are something a lot of folks back home might find impressive, except that those are ammunition weapons, and right now *Aquitaine* and *Fribourg* are wedded to the Expeditionary architecture, so they won't want them. Same with titan bolts. Nifty but not game changing. What we want is knowledge. Trade goods will be lists of things and examples I send home to draw out merchants in civilian hulls."

"Or traders here making the long sail?" she asked.

"Absolutely," he said. "That's why we have coordinates and some cultural notes about the closest systems for anyone who wants them."

"Because we're not a military threat?" she probed.

"Everybody is a military threat, Kaur," he said. "But we captured the *Fribourg Empire* with trade. We'd like to do the same here. That's why the First Lord of the Fleet sent me. To secure our last frontier with the best tools she had."

He watched her face for clues. They had rounded more than once on this subject like bulldogs on a bone, but she didn't have the authority to do things and had always held back from certain topics. He assumed military things that this new Director would handle, and Phil was fine with that.

Heavy footsteps at high speed approaching. Bodyguards around him tensing and then relaxing.

Phil turned to see Markus double-timing it across the patio with a comm in one hand.

"*Ground Control,*" he said with a bit of a gasp as he handed it off, so the man must have run all the way from the reception itself.

"This is Phil," he said into the device as he held it to his ear.

"Phil, are you alone?" Heather asked simply, voice hard and clipped.

Something was wrong.

"Kaur Singh is standing next to me," he replied. "What happened?"

"We have a problem…"

CHAPTER TWENTY-EIGHT

"Hey, that's weird."

Heather looked up. She was on the bridge today, instead of in an office doing paperwork, mostly because she had somehow managed to get it all done.

For today.

"What's weird, Leyla?" she asked.

Heather noted that almost every head had perked up and looked around like a field of prairie dogs.

Senior Centurion Leyla Ekmekçi didn't do *weird*.

Didn't help when the woman put her face down and started typing furiously rather than answer the question. Heather unbuckled and rose, walking over to her Science Officer in case she needed to poke the woman.

Everyone was on pins and needles right now. With Phil on the surface, she didn't need the extra stress, although as practical jokes went, Leyla might have found the perfect one. All she had to do was look up and say "Never mind…" and that would be that.

Except she was still typing.

"Talk, woman," Heather said in a louder voice. Maybe a little gruff.

"Tracking an orbital path," Leyla said obscurely.

As if that explained everything.

There were tens of thousand things in orbit of *Vilahana* that were at least the size of a human. More than seventy of them were starships that weren't permanently registered to *Vilahana*, but there were also minefields, junk yards, and orbital stations ranging from smaller than one of *Urumchi's* administrative shuttles all the way up to *Vilahana One*.

Finally, the woman looked up. Her normally dark face had gone pale. She slipped a few long hairs back over her ear from where they had fallen forward and took a breath.

"We got a problem," she announced.

"Combat imminent?" Heather asked, starting at the top and working her way down.

"Not that I can tell," Leyla said, shaking herself once, like she'd nearly frozen as she sat there staring at her screens. "Got a rock moving out of where it should be."

"Okay?" Heather pressed. "You could talk in whole paragraphs, you know?"

"Sorry," Leyla said. "I am tracking a big rock that normally follows a kind of wavelength path around *Vilahana's* solar orbit, sometimes closer to the star, sometimes farther out. It's kind of a captured moon, but it doesn't orbit *Vilahana*."

"What's it doing now?"

"Somehow, it got knocked out of its normal orbit," she replied. "Slowed down enough to become a navigational risk, except that we're beyond that. Heather, if I'm right it's going to impact on the planet."

"Oh, shit," Heather said. "Can we kill it?"

"It's more than sixteen kilometers across," Leyla said. "And scans like a solid lump of iron. If we had a week, probably Iveta could carve off enough pieces to deflect it using the Fours, but my read-out says we're looking at an impact midday tomorrow."

"Where?"

"What?"

"Where will it hit, Centurion?" Heather let her voice turn hard now. Leyla was floundering into an emotional state. "Give me coordinates."

"Stand by," Leyla replied, snapping to again.

Heather looked around.

"Don't bring us to combat footing, but let the corvettes know to stop one step short," she said loudly. "Let flag bridge handle it and roust them. Since Phil and Harinder are both planetside, route their comm through me with the flag."

Nods and assents.

"That can't be right," Leyla muttered, like she'd found a way to top her earlier practical joke.

It would have, but none of them were laughing right now.

"Close enough to dead center on Fryany Port, Command Centurion," Leyla said. "Just after lunch-time local."

About the time that everyone was supposed to sit down and start chatting in a semi-formal stance, after Patte and then Phil gave speeches.

"Flag Bridge, find me Phil immediately," Heather called out. "Leyla, get me as specific and detailed as you can, so we can let everyone know."

"I've got Dunklin on an encrypted line," someone said over the intercom. "He's en route to the First Centurion now."

"This is Phil," the man came on the line in under thirty seconds.

"Phil, are you alone?" Heather asked simply, trying not to give anything away, even encrypted.

If that was possible.

"Kaur Singh is standing next to me," Phil said a little evasively. "What happened?"

"We have a problem," Heather said. "There is an asteroid in near-*Vilahana* orbit that has been moved from where Leyla expected it. It will hit the planet in about eighteen hours, more or less on your coordinates."

There was a long pause.

"Moved?" he asked.

"You think that noon tomorrow is random luck, Phil?" Heather snapped.

"Negative, *Ground Control*," he replied tightly. "Confirming. Can you send everything you have to *Aranyani*? Their boom is on the surface and we can trust their systems right now."

"Leyla is packaging it as we speak, but you need to have them sit on it if Kaur isn't right there," she said. "Why don't I beam it to Markus and let him use the projector in his backpack."

"Yes, do that as well, but start calculating evacuation routes," Phil said. "I presume you can't deflect it?"

"Not in the time we've got, Phil."

"Okay," he said simply. "Start thinking outside the box and let me know if anyone has anything that might work. I'm going to go ruin the Governor's day."

CHAPTER TWENTY-NINE

Kaur watched Phil, listening to only half the conversation. It did not sound auspicious.

He closed the communicator and stared at her for a long moment before glancing around. They were alone on this section of the patio, not counting the musicians in the distant corner and Phil's combat team.

"There is an asteroid on a collision course with *Vilahana*," he said quietly. "Estimated impact midday tomorrow. I presume most people missed it because everyone landed their senior officers and booms on the surface. Heather doesn't think there is anything we can do to deflect it in the eighteen hours we have to prevent this."

Kaur went cold all over. All the booms could escape easily enough, including *Aranyani* and *Khandoba*, the Ship of the Line that had transported Director Narang to the conference. But there was a much larger population here, not just citizens of Fryany Port, but farmers farther out. Even if they could be evacuated, where would they go?

Vilahana was not a densely populated planet, but ten million people would overwhelm the capacity at hand, as well as the orbital platforms that might hold some.

"What are we doing?" Kaur asked, falling into step next to Phil as he started to move.

"We are going to probably start an unfortunate panic, Kaur," he replied. "There is no easy way to tell people this. You need to let Arya Chaudhari know that Heather is sending her information. Is there any way you can think of to deflect an iron-heavy asteroid sixteen kilometers across?"

They were on the stairs now, rattling heavily with all the armed men and women around them.

"A Pressor Beam might do it," she replied. "But we don't have any ships equipped with such a thing. We've experimented with using them to deflect and destroy missiles, as an extension of a Shield Projector, but they aren't that accurate."

"Pressor Beam?" Phil asked, stopping cold at the bottom of the stairs. "Against that much mass?"

"It could probably be done, but I would have to ask Nam to look it up," Kaur said. "Not anything high on my list."

"That's your immediate task, then," he said. "Find me some answers and let Heather and Leyla know."

She didn't mind the man issuing orders right now. It would be when Director Narang and Governor Patte sought to override Phil Kosnett that there would be issues.

They would lose that argument.

"What can they do?" Kaur asked.

"If this is sabotage, *Mischief* as we call it in the *Aquitaine* Navy, then someone did it," Phil said. "If my people know what they're looking for, they can tell me who did it."

"Very good," she said, coming to a decision. "I will return to *Aranyani* immediately and prep for evacuation liftoff while you talk to Patte. If we assume sabotage, do we also presume an assassination attempt against you, since you only have those little shuttles?"

That rocked the man. But he wasn't used to thinking of himself as a man who moved stellar nations, all rumors, legends, and stories to the contrary.

"Maybe," Phil said, turning to her. "If acceptable, I'll catch a ride to orbit with you, and we'll do it shortly, rather than wait. I know we can't get everyone, but maybe we can calculate the radius of destruction and figure out where to put camps."

"How do you calculate something like this, Phil?" she asked, aghast, even as they started moving again.

"*Buran* dropped an anti-matter torpedo on *St. Legier*, the Imperial Capital world, nine years ago this coming winter, Kaur," he said, striding through the first hallway and past guards coming to attention. "It was larger than your Ship of the Line *Khandoba*. *Aquitaine* has a very good understanding of how much damage such an explosion might generate."

She nodded and split down a side hallway, pulling her own comm and opening a line to Arya.

"We have a problem…"

CHAPTER THIRTY

Phil let his marines punch the hole he needed in the crowd, scowling and growling at folks to clear a path through to the governor. The small woman in the lead did an exceptional job, using her petiteness to convince bigger men to give way.

The snarl on Phil's face when people looked over her shoulder probably helped.

He felt like a gravity well, from the way a number of folks had drifted into his purposeful wake.

Patte noticed the approach and possibly expected barbarian cavalry charging over a hill from the way he turned completely white. Kaur had vanished, but that just meant she had a head start on getting to a transport to take her to the starport and start coordinating with both ships.

"First Centurion?" Patte asked as Phil stopped a polite distance away and bowed his head to the his host.

"We have a situation, Governor," Phil said loud enough for others nearby to pick up.

Might as well make this clean and clear now, so there was less time spent fixing transcription errors later.

Patte got serious, which was good. He had already been

working to tone down all the exclamation points, so maybe he would turn into a decent leader at some point.

Or would have, had somebody not decided to make an example of his planet.

Phil drew a breath and stood up tall.

"I am given to understand from my vessel in orbit that something had deflected a large asteroid from its normal solar orbit in the vicinity of *Vilahana*," Phil said simply, not allowing any emotion into his voice. No *accusation*.

Not yet, anyway.

Patte went blank for a moment.

"Meaning?" he asked.

"Meaning that they think it will intercept the planet sometime tomorrow," Phil continued. "With *catastrophic* effects."

"What do we do?"

The man was starting to get emotional. Hysterical, even. Phil couldn't blame him, but needed the man at least a little stable now.

"We need to calculate the time and location of possible impact, and begin evacuating everyone to a safer place," Phil explained. "It is apparently coming out of the sun, and targeted for Fryany, midday tomorrow. At least that is the first calculation. My team is working with *Aranyani* to refine that."

"How could you do this?" the man shrieked.

Others around them started rumbling ominously enough that Phil's petite, feminine killer actually turned away from the Governor to look at a captain nearby. No doubt sizing him up for a hard takedown.

"I didn't, Governor," Phil said, letting his voice get enormous to override all the muttering. "*Aquitaine* doesn't have the technology to do something like this."

Technically not true, but Keller had done it once by attaching replacement drives from a couple of snubfighters to a much smaller rock in order to deflect it enough to hit a pirate base.

"THEN HOW???" Patte demanded.

"Someone suggested that a Pressor Beam could manage it," Phil said, quieter now as the voices had abated. "*Aquitaine* doesn't use such technology, but I've tasked *Aranyani* with figuring out who has recently. And who has spent any significant time in the vicinity of that rock to be able to secretly deflect it."

Phil paused and rotated on one heel to catch the eye of all the men and women around him.

"And when I find that person, I will take him or her into custody and deal with them," Phil announced angrily.

What punishment such a person might face was left to the imagination, but nobody here would expect that it would turn into a simple fine plus loss of trade rights.

Until six months ago, most nations in the cluster probably would have just tut-tutted at the thought that a pirate haven like *Vilahana* managed to get on somebody's bad side and ended up destroyed. Today, it was possibly one of the most important systems in the cluster. *Aditi* and *Ellariel* probably understood that, but not many other cultures would.

Phil let his threat sink in. Nobody flinched under his words. Any more than necessary, at least.

His pivot brought him back to Patte.

"You should activate all your emergency plans, Governor," Phil said, glancing at the others. "My people will provide you with all our scans and keep everyone updated as we learn more. *Urumchi* does not land a boom like most of you do, so I would ask that you consider assisting the evacuation as best you can."

"What will you be doing?" Patte demanded, but in a quieter voice.

Not shattered, but far less coherent than he'd been this morning.

"I'm going up there to see what I can do to stop it."

CHAPTER THIRTY-ONE

GUBERNATORIAL PALACE, VILAHANA

Kaur watched some booms immediately make for sky, while others began coordinating with ground services to perhaps evacuate people either to one of the stations or to what was hopefully a safe spot on the planetary surface. From the transponders, the aid was coming from locals and diplomats, while the ones best considered pirates of some flavor were fleeing immediately.

She looked around her bridge and caught Arya's eye.

"Assume that someone might attack us in lift-off," she said simply. "Coordinate with Heather and have them overhead and parked close to our secondary hull in orbit. All of them."

Arya gulped and went back to her tasks. Kaur turned to Nam next.

"What do we know about Pressor Beams, Nam?" she asked

On the ground, the woman didn't have any significant tasks, and Kosnett was still several minutes out.

"It's just orbital geometry, Commander," Nam replied. "Solar wind, gravity interactions, and time."

"Assume that whatever happened came after *Urumchi* arrived," Kaur said. "Nobody else would have a reason before then."

"Yes, Commander," Nam said. "Will let you know."

Kaur leaned back and studied things. Jagadish was hard at work prepping for flight, always something of an adventure in an atmosphere. It would be worse today, with so many ships all likely filling the skies at the same time. At least she could deploy the Shield Projector up like an umbrella while she flew. Anyone maneuvering to threaten her in any way would be immediately suspect.

And nobody else knew how deep into an atmosphere those enormous beams off *Urumchi* could reach, if Heather and her crew had a reason to kill somebody.

"Signal from Kosnett," Arya called. "Two minutes out."

"Misra, start your launch sequence," Kaur called. "Nam, be ready for combat. All hands to battle stations."

That was a rare call from the ground, though not impossible. In the past, it was usually the result of hostile forces coming out of jump on a raid, and Kaur being caught on the ground. Today, it might be the same, without knowledge of who might be attacking.

"Get me a line to Heather," she called.

"Iveta on the comm, Commander," Arya replied immediately. "She has tactical."

Tactical.

Yes, Heather would have already turned over control. *Aquitaine* was strange that way, having their command centurion turn over command to their first officer for fighting, but Kaur supposed that it would let her concentrate on bigger things, while Arya focused exclusively on guns and maneuver.

"Iveta, this is Kaur Singh," she announced. "We will be lifting in approximately four minutes."

"Understood, *Aranyani*," the woman replied with a tone that almost sounded eager. "All vessels have been warned from your flight path and my weapons systems are unlocked. Escorts are currently dropping low into the atmosphere to escort you out."

How low? From the architecture, none of those ships were

ever designed to land on a planetary surface. However, if you had enough engine power, anything was possible, she supposed. And *Aranyani's* boom would be carrying their commander to orbit, so they would likely be pushing the envelope in a number of directions right now to make sure he was safe.

"Jagadish, as soon as Phil is confirmed aboard, warn off everyone else and launch when as they are safely clear of the pad," Kaur ordered.

Also rude, as you were supposed to give ground crews several minutes to get to safety, but *Aranyani* needed to push as well.

"Understood, Commander," he replied firmly. "Have been in communication with them to let them know."

Good, Jagadish was ahead of the curve on this. Time was of the essence. Worst case, she could shuttle Phil to safety and then return to get Patte or whoever showed up. Her cruiser could carry a few hundred extra people for a few weeks without stretching resources. Long enough to know what the next stage of the crisis might be.

Not enough to save *Vilahana*, but enough to make a difference in a few lives.

And Phil needed to be in orbit as soon as possible. *Aranyani* might need to remain there as well. A person deflecting the asteroid—and the chances of this timing being accidental were impossible—might want to attack *Urumchi*. That suggested they would need a fleet, because she would be close by, even if *Khandoba* remained aloof from battle.

"Stand by to launch," Jagadish called from his station.

That meant Phil was aboard, with his embassy, however many of the ambassadors had stayed with him. Or would each ambassador take the opportunity to ride to orbit with other ships, deepening the connections?

Again, Kaur could sense the future history of the Balhee Cluster turning, like a river running into an immoveable mountain and seeking a new path around it.

They lifted a little softer and smoother than normal, but

there would be folks aft who weren't used to this type of travel, as they had arrived aboard tiny shuttles, rather than the forward third of a starship.

"Nam, what is weapon status?" Kaur called.

"Everything charged before flight, Commander," her Weapons Officer replied. "Obviously, we can't handle recharging titan bolts or the Power Tap without losing engine power, but all generators are running, so we have the ability to keep the capacitors topped off if we need Main Guns or Point Guns."

"Rely on *Urumchi* and Beridze," Kaur decided. "If combat breaks out, we run like hell for orbit, keeping the Shield Projector and the engines as priority. Do not slow down for anything until after we dock. Questions?"

"No, Commander," Jagadish and Nam said in unison.

Kaur sat back and watched the horizon fall on the main screen.

"First Centurion and Flag Centurion approaching the bridge," one of her combat teams called.

"Let them in," Kaur ordered.

She needed Phil and Harinder up here, just in case. The entire *Aquitaine* squadron, minus only *Viking*, was above her as they climbed in a gigantic hollow cylinder all by themselves. But Iveta had warned everyone to stand clear, probably under threat of dismemberment by *Aquitaine* beams.

That woman would not issue casual threats.

Phil and Harinder entered and took up the same spots they had when *Tango* and *Saluki* had gotten frisky. Six weeks, but it felt like a lifetime ago.

"Status?" he asked.

"Climbing under protection of your escort squadron," Kaur replied.

Phil nodded and fell silent, watching without offering any additional commentary or even orders.

"Arya, where is *Khandoba*?" Kaur asked.

"Still on the ground, Commander," she replied.

Huh. Likely the Director was standing next to Patte and listening to that man's fears. Hopefully, nobody would end up blaming *Aquitaine* or the *Aditi Consensus* for this, although rumors would always fly faster than the truth.

And hopefully, it would be possible to deflect something so massive, although Kaur didn't think even Type-4 beams would do the trick.

They had to come up with something, though, or a planet might die.

CHAPTER THIRTY-TWO

Heather didn't assume any friendlies except *Aranyani* right now, including the other *Aditi* vessel, that monstrous Ship of the Line *Khandoba*. Everyone had been ordered clear of Phil's flight path, and she had ordered Iveta to shoot first and apologize later.

Possibly not the wisest option, given her Tactical Officer, but anybody giving them any reason right now had already decided to be trouble.

Too bad Barnaby wasn't here. *Viking* was just as heavily armed as *Urumchi*, and an extra pair of Fours that would let them take even *Khandoba* down if they had to.

But Heather assumed that the *Aditi Consensus* wanted to be friendly. As did a number of other ships that were moving their secondary hulls out to what Iveta had declared was a safe distance.

"Hey, that's odd," Leyla said under her breath, but Heather was already that keyed up.

"Talk to me," she called.

"Going back through my records, since we have all those scans," Leyla replied. "Think I got a match."

"Who?"

"Transponder identified them as *Wulfa*," Leyla said. "*Ingham Syndicate* armed transport, whatever that means."

"Galleon-sized or caravel?" Heather asked, defaulting to the pattern of ships the *Aditi Consensus* used with galleons being about the size of cruisers and caravels being more like frigates.

"Caravel," Leyla said. "They came out of Jump on April 3, spent a little time in orbit, flew out to our rock and were there for most of a day, and then flew back, before departing two days later."

"Give me their scan on the main screen," Heather called.

The image of the stars shifted to a three dimensional rendering of a small hull that tended to follow the *Dalou Hegemony* lines, but not quite. Like someone had stolen some plans and built them elsewhere, or modified some design to look *Dalou* from a distance.

Twin engines out horizontal on pylons. Stubby body leading to a short, thick neck. Wider head that always looked to Heather like a dragon pouncing. *CC-501* was next to it for scale, with the corvette being about a quarter shorter and nowhere near as wide on the deck plain.

"Firebird on the bow mount?" she asked.

"Negative," Leyla said. "Not sure what it is."

"Ask Arya on a secured line," Heather ordered.

"Stand by."

Heather studied the ship. Looked like simple Main Guns on the wing mounts, but she'd seen enough Syndicate ships to know that almost every one brought a different option to battle, depending on what they thought they might need. For some it was titan bolts or the modifications known as firebirds. Others might add missile racks. Some just added more beams and called it good.

She assumed that the Syndicates would be the first to start mounting pulse weapons, once they laid hands on them. Organized navies usually liked to design new ships, like the modified, second-generation Expeditionary Heavy Dreadnought she was commanding, to take advantage of the Pulse-Two.

"Arya says high confidence that it is a jury-rigged Pressor Beam on the centerline mount," Leyla called. "Nobody saw it in action, and the design is still experimental, but that might be it."

"We only need to convince a grand jury," Heather replied. "Someone else can convict. Confirm that they are gone?"

"Affirmative," Leyla said. "Did the dirty and left."

"Anybody else from *Ingham Syndicate* still around?" Heather pressed.

"*Tango*, with Utkin down on the surface and probably lifting soon," Leyla replied. "Then two ships escorting his secondary hull, currently on a trailing orbit just above our horizon."

"Show me their readouts," Iveta interrupted.

Technically, Iveta was in charge, but there was no shooting, so she'd been quiet. Shooting things might be happening soon enough though…

Tango Heather recognized, with the boom section currently showing as a separate piece on the display because it was still on the surface. In the old days, roughly a big light cruiser for size, but not as big as a *Founder*-class. Next to it was a close cousin of *Saluki*, what the Syndicates apparently called a *Picket*. *Maddog* reminded her of a light frigate from the old days when the Empire built them in wolfpack raiding squadrons.

In between was a heavy destroyer, but nothing like Alber' had flown. Bigger than the Republic used to build them, but that was inefficiency of tech and design, rather than an indication of firepower. As you got more advanced, your ships could get smaller for the same guns, or add more power and more weapons. *Atlas* was a *Raider*-class, whatever that meant, but Heather assumed that those were the ships that preyed on convoys, with *Pickets* as escorts and spotters, while big ships like *Tango* were called *Enforcers* for a reason.

"Both *Maddog* and *Atlas* are combat-ready?" Iveta asked.

"Both have their booms attached, yes," Leyla replied. "Neither was down on the surface, for what that's worth."

"I'll assume until proven otherwise that they knew it was coming, as did *Tango*, and they have just been looking for an excuse," Heather said. "I have the flag. Comm, get me Galia Abbasi on the line. In fact, get everyone and lock them in now, just so we're ready when the flag goes up."

Heather ignored the big screen and concentrated on her personal one as faces began to appear around the outside, including Iveta who was all of three meters away.

Galia Abbasi appeared quickly. Command Centurion, *CC-501*. Command Corvette. The role Kigali had fulfilled for Jessica and *First Expeditionary*, back during the wars.

"What do we know?" Galia asked as she came on.

Like Aliza Babatunde, Galia was of an ethnotype called African Diaspora from the early days of starflight, with dark eyes and graying black hair kept short. Senior among the escorts because Heather had asked for her specifically, going back to their Academy days.

"We know there are things unseen, Galia," Heather replied. "I want you to detach *Task Force 502* like before and move them to a spot where they can hit the three *Ingham* ships or intercept if they go after *Aranyani*'s boom."

She turned to the image of Erle Kuiper, Command Centurion of *CB-502*. Battle Corvette. Erle was as fair as Galia was dark, but she wasn't Chinese Diaspora, instead being Korean, originally. Heather was always a little fuzzy about the difference, but both groups considered it significant, so she just ran with it.

"Erle, if trouble erupts, you protect Phil," Heather ordered. "Then *Aranyani* if he's not aboard us. Anybody shoots, you go for his throat. If I want to, I'll jerk your chain back, but don't assume that you have to play nice, as long as you don't shoot first without a good reason. Questions?"

"You want your signature etched into anybody's hull?" the woman asked with a grin.

"No, but I reserve the right to change my mind later," Heather laughed. "Shift now and take command of your Task Force under my flag."

"*Task Force 502* in motion," Erle announced.

Her image froze, so Heather assumed the woman was reaching out to her new team to organize things. Hopefully, Harinder would be available shortly. She had the touch with these sorts of things. Heather just planned on issuing orders for now and letting Phil's people handle things until she had to adjust.

She wasn't another Jessica Keller, and had no interest in ever spending that much time on tactical and strategic combat planning. She was *Ground Control.* That meant keeping everyone else sorted out for now.

At least until it was time to shoot things.

CHAPTER THIRTY-THREE

Phil watched on Kaur's screen as things got sorted. Heather had gone ahead and put *502* and her support on a wing that just happened to be between *Aranyani* and the *Ingham* ships. Not accidental, so he assumed that they knew something they weren't telling yet.

Viking was out scouting, but that still left him the core of the fleet he'd been expecting to sail dangerous seas with. Time to put all that power to use.

"Do we know anything?" he asked the room, quietly enough that they could ignore him if they wanted.

"Heather and Leyla have a scan of an *Ingham* ship that spent time around the target asteroid about a month ago," the Sub-Commander replied evenly. "We're guessing, but it appeared to mount what looks like a Pressor Beam on their centerline."

Heather and Leyla? Had everyone gotten to that level of informality?

Phil supposed so. They had been working closely together for more than six weeks now, since *Urumchi* had stopped the *Ingham* pirates from whatever they might have done to an *Aditi Consensus* cruiser they had trapped.

And a Pressor Beam on a ship that was in the right vicinity

just meant that they thought they could get away with it. He made a note to chat with Aliza when they all got back to *Urumchi*. She was aft right now with about half of her ambassadors, the other half making plans to join other ships in an official capacity.

Aliza would need to notify everyone that *Ingham* was likely the suspect. Both *Aditi* and *Aquitaine* would be at the hot end of rumors, so Aliza would need to up her public relations game to offset those negative stories. But they were trained and prepared for that sort of thing.

"*Ingham* behaving?" Phil followed up.

"So far." Chaudhari turned and smiled at him. "Iveta threatened anybody approaching us during flight, plus all the corvettes are in escort and intercept positions."

"Have we refined the impact timing and location?" he asked.

Why not go for broke? Heather and the others had been sitting in overwatch. Maybe they had learned something.

"We still think early afternoon tomorrow, First Centurion," Chaudhari replied. "Close enough to Fryany for government work."

Yeah, this was not an accident. More like an assassination attempt, but Phil couldn't see who was the target, unless Utkin or his bosses had decided to eliminate Patte as a source of support for a new galactic order. Phil could always build stations and bases in orbit. However, if an explosion and impact that big happened, *Aquitaine* would spend the better part of a decade just repairing and rebuilding to make the planet safe and habitable again.

That would be someone else's job, though, because if *Ingham* did it on purpose, their entire existence was forfeit. He would apply *Aquitaine* Naval Law at that point, which still remembered *Sentient* warships in orbit dropping massive asteroids on planets as a way to destroy factories and populations.

Excepting the Librarian at *Ballard*, *Sentience* was illegal. Period. As was attacking the surface of an inhabited planet with bolide weapons. Keller had gone after an illegal pirate base that way, but had also allowed the few people at the base to surrender and be evacuated well ahead of time.

Maybe what Phil needed was to go ahead and upgrade himself to *RAN Kongō* one of these days, just so he could put all his experience with piracy to work. He already had *Ground Control* and *Stunt Dude* handy. Somewhere *Lady Blackbeard* was commanding another *Scorpion*-class corvette. He couldn't get the whole gang back together, but Phil Kosnett had also just spent three years teaching Advanced Piracy to a bunch of hungry *Aquitaine* officers who would love to put that training to use.

"Do we have a secured comm line to *Urumchi*?" he asked around the other conversations about lifting off, but Chaudhari was paying attention.

"Affirmative," she said. "Open or on a line?"

"Open is fine," Phil replied. "I don't have any secrets from you or the *Consensus* today."

He caught the look out of the corner of Kaur's eye, but it was simple truth. They would all need to work together if they were going to find a way through this mess.

"Go ahead."

"Heather, this is Phil. The password is Saxon," he said. "Have Leyla and Isabèl Pan on *CM-507* start hard-scanning the rock. I need you to know as much as possible about it when I dock in an hour, so we can start eliminating ideas and focus on the ones that might work."

"Already ahead of you, Phil," she replied. "Will get Isabèl on it as well, but she's in my hip pocket right now."

"Understood," Phil noted. "Stand by for fleet maneuvers with the *Aditi Consensus* for the time being."

"Roger that."

Phil nodded to Arya Chaudhari to cut the line and caught the look of surprise on a number of faces.

"We will do this together, or not at all, my friends," he

announced simply. "No politics. No borders. Just people in need."

Kaur nodded back at him, but Phil could tell that something had changed. *Aquitaine* and the *Aditi Consensus* would be working together to solve an intractable problem. *Dalou* and *Gloran* would have to decide whether to help or be left out, as would *Ewin* and any other *Zen-Mekyo Syndicate* commanders in the area.

There was no way in hell he was letting *Ingham* have his back right now.

CHAPTER THIRTY-FOUR

INGHAM ENFORCER TANGO

Basant Utkin forced himself to remain still and quiet while his crew went through the process of launching *Tango*'s boom with an extra seventy-seven evacuees that he was supposed to haul to *Vilahana One* in orbit. Important families with connections to *Ingham*. People he would need to spread all his rumors about how suspicious it was that *Aquitaine* blew up *Vilahana*.

Even if the truth came out eventually, people would always wonder, as long as he had prepared the field with lies and innuendo ahead of time. Because if *Aquitaine* got a foothold here, they would change everything forever.

"Mati, bring a map up on the screen," Basant finally said, just to break the tense silence. "Quarter Planetary Orbit Vertical."

Matvei Ignatiev, *Tango*'s Pilot. He glanced back, nodded, and typed with his off-hand while still climbing for deep space. Next to him, Gauhar Aigul sat with all her weapons ready. Basant would not provoke a confrontation with a warfleet before he was docked with his secondary hull and able to flee. Maybe not even then, but he needed to be prepared.

Three of the *Aquitaine* escorts were suspiciously between

Tango's squadron and the *Aditi* cruiser boom, but nobody was shooting, so they must not know the truth. Probably just being prepared, since *Tango* had been the last person to start a rumble in orbit.

Before Basant understood that the *Aquitaine* vessels were so dangerous.

Saluki would never fight again. The Directorate had ordered it flown back to a secret base to be stripped, just so *Ingham* engineers could see what sort of damage those stuttering Main Guns did. Most of the crew had been removed and spread out across Basant's squadron, leaving behind only enough crew to fly it somewhere later.

But they were under strict orders to not provoke the strangers or the *Consensus*. That would just be suicide. The only standing order they had was to run like hell if anyone came after them, but to surrender rather than be destroyed. The Directorate could always pay the usual ransom or trade with captured crews to get them back later.

"How soon to dock?" Basant asked the back of Mati's head.

"Seventy minutes, unless you need me to cut corners," the man called back.

Basant considered it. Plotted out all the moves he had been expecting.

Aquitaine had reacted faster and surer than he had thought they would. Apparently they had been scanning more than just the local vicinity and any possible foes. They claimed to be surveyors and explorers, but Basant had of course discounted that entirely, expecting a rival clan.

They had outthought him.

Basant needed to make sure that they didn't do that again. The Directorate didn't understand just how dangerous these strangers were. How much was going to change.

How quickly everyone needed to update their thinking.

Basant considered loading up another Salvager like *Wulfa* with supplies, or maybe just take her with him and head to

Aquitaine, where they could trade directly and try to acquire these new weapons.

Someone would trade. They always did, money under the table while making loud protestations of honesty.

The louder the denials, usually the easier the deals.

But *Tango*, *Maddog*, and *Atlas* didn't stand a chance against the combined force over there. He needed to elude them, drop off his passengers, and get to the edge of the gravity well. From out there, he could flee faster than they could catch him. Patte and the others would just have to deal.

Basant drew a hard breath. He'd set everything in motion, but this was only the opening move in a much longer and more complicated game.

"Mati, cut those corners," he ordered loudly. "In fact, get us to the station first and as fast as you can so we can drop everyone off. Order the squadron to rendezvous with us there for docking, and pay attention to what *Aquitaine* does in response."

"Understood," Mati replied.

Basant leaned back and wondered what the cluster would look like a year from now.

CHAPTER THIRTY-FIVE

Heather looked up when Leyla spoke over the usual noise of people talking on the bridge.

"*Tango*'s boom just changed course and announced to everyone that they were going to dock with the big orbital station before mating with their *Energiya* module," Leyla said.

"*Task Force 502*, maintain your mission," Heather ordered.

Aranyani's boom was higher up, closer to space, but still a bit from docking. Iveta had an open zone for people to navigate around, but that wasn't going to impact the pirates much.

"Anybody else acting suspicious?" Heather asked.

"Chickens with heads cut off can be mistaken for wild beasts with murderous intent," Leyla replied.

"Helpful," Heather noted sarcastically.

"Pointing out the obvious, boss," Leyla chuckled from her corner. "Oh, signal from Isabèl."

Heather brought it up on her screen and pulled out a headset. There was a lot of noise right now as people kept everyone up to date and chatted constantly with Harinder's folks aft.

"Go ahead," Heather said as Isabèl's image got crisp and live.

Isabèl was a tiny woman, barely 157cm tall. She shaved her

head daily, showing off golden skin and eyes almost the same hue.

"So I might be imagining things," the woman said in her low, quiet voice. "But I'm picking up a haze over there right now. Nothing to compare it to, but it might be a quiet minefield, command controlled with passive, short-range sensors. We've been studying how *Vilahana* does it, so I've learned some nifty new things you can do, if we ever want Lady Moirrey to make us something crazy."

Centurion Moirrey *zu* Kermode. Heather had actually served with her and met the woman a few times, while she was something of a demigod to most people these days. But when it came time to make weapons, that might be an appropriate description.

"Clues?" Heather asked.

"Every rock out there had some level of gravity, Heather," she said. "Smaller rocks that float nearby because they've been captured or at least gravitationally entangled. Maybe a small impact chipped off some rocks. Something. Our target has a bunch of rocks around them, all flying together."

"Okay?" Heather asked as a placeholder, unsure of the meaning.

"If this rock was recently jarred out of its stable orbit, those wouldn't still be around," Isabèl replied. "And there wouldn't have been time for new ones to spall off. Not in a month."

"But if that *Ingham* ship spent a day there..." Heather said, seeing where Isabèl was going.

"They might have dropped mines as well, knowing that they had time for the flight to stabilize," she agreed. "Maybe even programmed them to deploy after a week, so as to get the right momentum, and are quietly station-keeping with short-range point lasers to talk to each other."

"How close do you have to get to identify?" Heather asked.

"Not sure," Isabèl replied. "We haven't actually caused one to fire, so we don't know what they do. If it was me, I'd mix beams, bombs, and missiles about evenly, just to mess with people."

Heather considered her options. All bad, but she had sharp people willing to try things.

"As soon as *Aranyani* docks, you swing out and look for a corner on that field where you might engage and be ready to run like hell," Heather ordered. "We'll all be moving that direction as a group, so you'll have support, but every second might count if someone doesn't want us getting too close."

"Suppose they attached engines to it, like Keller supposedly did?" Isabèl asked.

"Keller really did do that," Heather said. "Denis Jež, actually. I heard the story direct from her people. But we should have noticed something that big. The *Aditi* folks think that they used a device called a Pressor Beam. An extension of the logic of the Shield Projector."

"Gotcha," Isabèl nodded. "I'll start making plans. Do you want me to provoke it, if I can find a corner?"

"That's Phil's call," Heather replied. "I'll brief him when he gets here, and I will want you in position if he wants to move quickly."

"On it."

And she was gone.

Heather looked around, but everyone was face down on some task, trying to find a way to stop a giant, planet-killing asteroid and save the day.

If they could.

CHAPTER THIRTY-SIX

Phil checked the time. Supposedly fifteen hours to impact, give or take. They'd made good time to orbit and *Aranyani* was in the process of backing into the docking cradle of an *Energiya* module, although not nearly as gracefully as he'd watched *Buran* vessels do it, even under fire.

Aranyani still reminded him of a hand with three fingers, the boom section being longer and wider than the outer two, so that the rest of the ship almost looked like a horseshoe with it separated. *Urumchi* was above them in orbit, but moving closer now, to the point Phil might have thrown a rock and hit it. All three of his own Dragon-class Gunboats were out, and he was aware that a shuttle was hot to carry him and Harinder across, along with everyone else.

"Have you gotten any orders from your Director, Kaur?" he asked the Commander.

She turned and looked at him with hooded eyes.

"Not at present," she drawled carefully.

"I would greatly appreciate it if we could continue the current informal alliance we have been acting under before today, Commander Singh," he said just as carefully. "At least barring contrary orders from your superior at a future time."

She nodded.

"Understood, First Centurion," Kaur Singh replied. "What do you need?"

"I have no idea," Phil said. "But if Arya and Leyla can find something, we need to be able to move quickly to exploit whatever it is. We need to save *Vilahana* today. I'll settle for chasing someone down and breaking him tomorrow."

Her face got a little pained at his words, but Phil had done that on purpose. These people took a much more relaxed attitude to things like law enforcement than he would have. Phil understood why, but beavers allowed to nibble at the foundations of society had just reached the stage where a tree was going to fall on somebody's house.

Beavers didn't get to do that, so they would need to be moved somewhere else. Somewhere that didn't risk hurting people. Or they might have to get hurt.

"Harinder?" he asked.

"We're ready to go, Phil," she replied. "Heather has the flag, pending your arrival, with a lot of balls in the air and poised."

He unbuckled and rose, nodding to everyone.

"I wanted to take a moment and thank all of you for your hospitality, *Aranyani*," he said louder. "It is my hope that we can reciprocate sometime, and continue to be friends and allies moving forward."

He moved before anyone could do more than blink in his wake, exiting the bridge and picking up his usual combat team escorts. Everyone else had been left aft, out of the way, with just him and Harinder so honored to fly on the bridge with Commander Singh.

Now, he had work to do.

The Professor was in the classroom, and it was final exam time.

The shuttle was prepped and loaded, with two seats by the hatch as he slid in and took one. The pilot closed everything up and opened the bay doors. Kaur had rolled *Aranyani* on her side, so that the bay was aimed right at *Urumchi*'s rear flight deck. Again, he could have crossed on personal thrusters if he wanted. At the same time, Phil understood that everyone was being extra paranoid today, with the possibility of an assassin in orbit.

Iveta would rain hull fragments out of the sky if anyone fired right now. Heather would probably point out pieces that needed a second shot.

It was nice, being loved.

Now he just needed to teach the people of the Balhee Cluster to respect him.

And maybe fear him just a little bit.

"Stand by for landing," the pilot said, almost as quickly as they lifted from *Aranyani*'s deck.

The shuttle shot quickly across the gap and got swallowed up in one of the Dragon flight bays, each an enormous space for such a tiny craft as he was flying in.

The bay went bright as the doors closed and pressure came up. The pilot had managed to almost bootlegger his landing, putting the hatch not that far from the airlock into *Urumchi* proper, so someone had briefed the man on his flight today.

Still impressive work.

"We have minimal acceptable pressure, First Centurion," the pilot announced. "Stand by for the hatch to open. There will be wind, so everyone be prepared."

Minimal acceptable pressure. Good enough to breathe, like standing atop a four-thousand-meter peak somewhere. The air raced out of the shuttle as the hatch opened. Phil was off quickly, thankful for the extra two minutes that the pilot had given him by not waiting for formal matching.

The airlock was opening as he approached, so they were all in on this.

"Harinder with me to flag bridge," Phil yelled over the sound of bodies pouring in his wake. "Everyone else to action stations."

Through hallways intentionally emptied of people, so he could get to his flag bridge quickly.

Heather was seated at the command table when he entered, forming a ninety degree corner as he and Harinder sat.

"*Task Force 502* is currently providing escort to the pirates," she said without preamble. "*CM-507* is surveying the asteroid from closer in, looking at what might be a minefield surrounding it to keep us from getting close. Is *Aranyani* friendly?"

"Allied until they get alternate orders, so move them around to watch *Tango* for now," Phil said. "I have the flag. Detach all of our shuttles from the entire squadron and let the Governor have them to evac people until I say otherwise. Bucket in a monsoon, but every life we save counts for something tomorrow. What do we know?"

"We have high confidence that an *Ingham* vessel used something like a Pressor Beam to move the rock in this direction," Heather said. "There might be a minefield protecting it. The ship we want to talk to is long gone, but the *Ingham Syndicate* has three others present, currently behaving but we outgun them by orders of magnitude."

"Watch them hard and let Iveta have them if they fire on anyone," Phil decided. "Get me all the Command Centurions on the link and add Kaur Singh as well."

Most of them were faces on his screen. A few were frozen but came live. Kaur was there a moment later.

"Okay, people," Phil announced. "You've had a few hours to think about it. No idea too crazy. What can we do to stop this rock?"

"The Type-4s might spall chunks off," Iveka said. "However, gaming it out suggests that the first shot causes it to start rolling and prevents us from being able to really carve away anything. Additionally, anything we break off still has momentum and is likely to impact the planetary surface, but over a wider area."

"Noted," Phil replied.

At least she'd gamed it out and come to the same conclusion he had. Now might be the one time when carrying the old Primaries would have been useful, since they focused everything on a tight pulse that might punch a hole pretty deep into a rock like this. Maybe not blow starlight through it, but something. And all that energy could have been calculated to hit like a rocket and push it off to one side.

If wishes were fishes.

"Did I understand correctly that there might be a minefield?" Kaur asked over the line.

"That's right," Leyla replied, also on the line with Arya, since sensors would be key to what was coming. "*CM-507* is close enough to pick some of them out now, but we don't know what they'll shoot back with."

"Can a Shield Projector clear mines?" Command Centurion Pan asked now, from her vista overlooking the thing.

"It can, but only if they used nothing except explosive mines," Kaur replied. "Which is why so many people mix explosives, beams, and missiles. You use the Projector like a snowplow at that point, but I would expect counterfire and incoming if you got too close."

Something niggled at the back of Phil's mind, but he couldn't wrap his hands around it.

"*507*, how hard to clear all that?" he asked instead.

Somebody didn't want him getting close, so that meant they feared what he could do if he did.

Ergo.

"Time and patience, as with all things, Phil," she replied.

"I don't have either right now," he replied. "Shift the entire squadron around to engage the mines with Type-3s. *Urumchi* and two escorts will hang back. *507*, don't do anything until we've got you protected with overlapping fields of defense."

"Roger that," she said.

"Iveta, when we get close, use the Fours, but keep an eye on anyone coming up behind us."

"I'll have your flank, First Centurion," Kaur spoke up. "We don't have the weapons to clear mines, but I can hold anyone else at bay."

"Thank you," Phil said. "*502*, you'll have point. *501*, pick your escorts for the corners. Iveta, you have tactical. Get us into battle with a minefield."

Faces grimaced and nodded. Nobody really knew what to expect, except that folks in this neighborhood used mines offensively as well as defensively.

Phil had seen parts of *Project Mischief,* back in the old days, when Kermode had explored such things, but the war had sped up quickly once Jessica really got going, so that nobody used them much anymore. Speed and beams. The heart and soul of The Expedition itself.

And *Buran* had never bothered, because they could use their Capriole drives to get around them.

Phil supposed it was a lost art, but maybe he would send a note home and ask *zu* Kermode or Bedrov to invent him a better Shield Projector. One that had the range to hammer on any missiles or snubfighters he found nearby.

Tomorrow's task.

Today, he had to stop a giant rock from destroying an entire planet.

And millions of innocent lives.

CHAPTER THIRTY-SEVEN

GOVERNOR ANNEN PATTE'S PALACE

Annen watched the big display screens from a ready room deep underground. Not deep enough to protect him from what was coming, but safe from most things.

Whoever had come for him this time was serious.

He turned to Director Narang. Took that man's measure.

Half-bald and gray. Big once, but starting to sag in on himself. Taller and lighter-skinned than Kaur Singh, he gave off the air of a man who had once been a big-shot Commander, before turning into Brass and becoming a politician.

Annen almost preferred Kosnett and Singh.

"What are they doing?" he demanded, aware that the man had an earpiece in and was getting a running commentary from his own ship's boom.

"Commander Singh reports the possibility of a minefield around the asteroid," he said in a deep voice. "The combined squadron is moving to investigate and see what they can do. I still suggest that you would be better suited to taking charge of the situation from one of the orbital platforms, Governor, or at least my flagship."

"Soon, Director," Annen replied. "We will depart in a few hours. That gives us time to escape."

"The *Aquitaine* ships are sending all of their shuttles down to help," the Director continued. "Several booms are also involved."

"I have ordered as many people to the far side of the planet as possible," Patte said. "When this is done, I will demand a formal inquiry. The *Aditi Consensus* and *Aquitaine* will be made to explain their parts in all this."

Personally, Annen didn't think any of them had any responsibility for this, but already rumors were flying. Some secret weapon Kosnett had brought, possibly to make himself look like a hero when he saved the day.

That was why Annen had remained behind, even as most of the important people had fled to orbit. Plus, he had the boom of an *Aditi* Ship of the Line as a personal chariot, assuming he didn't push Narang too far.

"We have had nothing to do with this, Governor," Narang replied nervously.

As if unsure what his subordinate might have done in the two months she had been here already. Narang had only been here a few days. Just enough to call on a few people and get ready for the formal gathering that was supposed to have begun in the morning.

Fat chance of that.

Still, if this was an assassination, perhaps the ground was the worst place to be.

"Director Narang, I have changed my mind," Annen said peremptorily. "We should move to orbit now, just so we have a better view of what is going on. How many people can you transport?"

"Your staff and others," the man replied with obvious relief. "Up to one hundred and fifty people."

"Excellent," Annen said, turning to some of his staff lingering nearby.

He nodded and they raced off, no doubt collecting bribes to allow people to join the fifty or sixty extra he would be able to take.

Much of Annen's wealth was off-world, staged in a variety of banks against that day in another few years when he abruptly retired and vanished, hopefully several steps ahead of whoever thought they might have words with him when that day came.

If all else failed, he could demand that *Khandoba* transport him to *Aditi* proper, where he could file formal complaints and then drift into the background, a former governor of a destroyed colony.

Because if that thing hit, *Vilahana* was unlikely to be habitable again in his lifetime.

It seemed like it would be a lot of effort at that point, just to kill the governor of a nowhere world.

CHAPTER THIRTY-EIGHT

Isabèl noted the way the rest of the team was stretched out behind her like an arrowhead pointed at the planet. *CM-507* at the center, with *Urumchi* directly aft and all the Guardians in wings backward.

"Prifti, you have Tactical," she reminded him.

Senior Centurion Agam Prifti tended to get wound in on himself. Minesweeping was a task of patience, like splitting diamonds, so the *measure twice, cut once* logic was pounded into everyone's souls.

"I have Tactical," Senior Centurion Prifti looked up and around. "Gunner, I have laid out an engagement sequence for the Three-X and the forward Pulse. You control those and I'll keep the Pulse-Two handy."

Isabèl noted the woman nod in response. Centurion Celeste Bellandini. The woman had long, curled, white hair and red eyes to go with her smooth, ghostly, white skin. It contrasted oddly to her tall bones and beefy build, but being an albino had never slowed the woman down. Just made her work harder than everyone else.

"Ready to fire," Celeste said quietly.

Like the rest of them, she did everything quietly. Isabèl had never been sure if that came with the job, or the job found people who thrived under such circumstances.

"Engage as you bear," Agam said.

The first shot hammered one of the larger nodes that they had found once they got closer. All of it was man-made, but grouped a lot tighter than the fields in *Vilahana's* orbit. But then, they weren't keeping people out, so much as punishing them for getting too close.

The mine exploded mightily. Instantly, several others disgorged missiles that had been passively tracking the squadron.

"I have inbound," Celeste said aloud.

"Guardians, clear your corners," the Flag Centurion said over the team channel.

CG-504 and *CG-506* opened up immediately with everything they had, like a tide attacking sand castles.

More missiles, as well as some of what Isabèl knew were the equivalent of Main Guns from some local ships. Type-3s, roughly, with good range but not as much focus.

507 was just station-keeping in retrograde, so all the extra power from the engines was in the forward array of shields right now, and those were already upgraded from a normal corvette.

Life in the face of minefields.

She watched Celeste move on to the next target. Agam had selected the biggest ones on the theory that they were either the most dangerous or maybe controller nodes for the rest.

"*Urumchi*, I need you to kill targets fifty-seven and eighty-one," Agam said over the line. "They are out of our range without getting too close."

Outside, explosions and beams rocked things as missiles kept emerging and dying.

Whoever had done this was all set to splatter one or two ships. Isabèl hesitated to think what would have happened if *Aranyani* or one of the local destroyers had gotten too close. *Urumchi* was probably safe, but they had Pulse-Twos on every corner that were great at keeping things from impacting.

And there were a plethora of Type-3-Pulse available, with no reason to spare the horses.

"All ships hold current gap," Agam ordered over the line.

Isabèl studied the updated map. Agam had taken a ragged bite out of this corner, like a kid with a bit of a snaggletooth chomping an apple.

"Gunner, take target eighty-six then seventeen then hold," Agam ordered.

Isabèl saw the two highlights as Celeste adjusted her aim. All the biggest ones on this side of the asteroid were blown up, and these two were the only ones left with purple tags because she and Agam hadn't been sure what they did. Nobody had fired titan bolts at them, just Main Guns.

Isabèl hoped that those three were their limits. They didn't have a lot of time here, so they were making up for precision with an overabundance of firepower.

"*Urumchi*, I have one other target for you, and then we should be set to kill the field from the inside," Agam said.

The dreadnought fired one immense beam and a target over the north pole of the asteroid flashed into plasma.

All of a sudden, the amount of radio chatter from the various mines dropped at least fifty percent.

"Gotcha," Agam hammered a fist on his console, making everyone jump.

Mostly because he normally talked with his hands, right up until they had to fire, then he became perfectly still, like a painted statue.

"Flag, this is Prifti, aboard *CM-507*," he said over the main line. "I have a path for the Guardians to move up and begin engaging. I think we have killed all the command nodes for the field. Everyone should still exercise caution, obviously."

"*507*, this is Kosnett," the First Centurion came back instantly. "Nicely done, people. Guardian force, move forward with *507* and kill anything that looks man-made you can scan. Look for boxes on the surface of the asteroid that might be the deployers and make sure they are empty as well."

Isabèl kept a watch on the engines as they slowed down their retrograde and let the big rock drift past them. Both Agam and Celeste were firing constantly now, but the missiles had fallen to almost nothing, as had the beams. Apparently, without the control nodes, the rest would only engage when you got too close. And nobody was getting too close.

She took control of a secondary scanner and aimed it at the back side of the rock, where Leyla had suspected the pirate left a box of mines for them. The asteroid was not tumbling hardly at all, so it kept the same face pretty much forward all the time, meaning the back would be towards the sun and away from anyone on *Urumchi* looking this way.

Again, malice aforethought.

"I have a shipping container on the surface," Isabèl announced. "Confirming that it is empty at present, but we will need to drop marines down at some point to take possession."

"Acknowledged, Isabèl," Kosnett replied. "If I had shuttles, I would do it now, but we can wait. See if you can find any external writing with optics."

"On it."

Above her, Agam and Celeste were clearing the skies as fast as the guns could track new targets and hit them from long range, so she dialed in. There was some writing, but it was at a bad angle. She would need to move the ship around for a better view, but only after Agam was done.

CHAPTER THIRTY-NINE

Phil owned the big asteroid. At least as much as you could when it was racing across space and big enough to demand right of way. He even had pictures of a shipping manifest painted on the side, written in a commercial code that he didn't have time or resources to crack today.

Another tomorrow problem. He felt like a cop pursuing a criminal conspiracy, but that also described more than half the vessels currently within scan range.

"Iveta and Leyla, confirm your latest report," Phil said, mostly just to be sure.

"Nothing the Fours can do would matter unless we had a week or more," Iveta spoke. She had Tactical right now, even though there was no fighting going on.

Just the cooling plasma and scattering rubble that had been a professionally-organized minefield an hour ago.

"Additionally, all the pieces we might blast off still have to land somewhere," Leyla tacked on.

"What we need is a Pressor Beam of our own," Heather said. "But nobody remembered to bring one to the party."

"I'll add it to the list for next time," Phil said, trying to sound like a jest, in spite of how serious things were.

If he wanted to look, he could see booms and shuttles flying all over the place, trying to get people to the back side of where that rock would hit, presumably with enough food and emergency shelters that they didn't perish in a week.

Every country craft that could fly was in motion as well, but they would run out of fingers long before he ran out of holes in the dyke he was facing.

"What I really need is a bigger Shield Projector," Phil groused out loud. "Something that could just push the damned thing far enough off line that it missed the planet entirely. Then we could deal with it at our leisure."

The faces around the edge of his screen nodded or commiserated.

But that thing in the back of his head kept tugging. Poking at him.

Shield Projectors were just specialized shield generators, like everyone used to protect themselves against various energies unleashed in modern combat. For local warships, they added an extra layer that could be spun around to face a specific threat.

Phil located the line he wanted and pressed the button.

"Engineering," a man replied. "Command Machinist El-Amin."

"Rais, it's Phil," he said. "How much could you reinforce the forward shield array, if I wasn't shooting at anybody else and needed the engines pushing?"

"Lots, First Centurion," El-Amin replied, still a little puzzled. "What are you facing? I thought we had a big rock."

"Can we just sidle up to that big rock and push it with the shields?" Phil asked.

He'd forgotten that the command line to all his ships was open. Eyes got huge as he watched.

Phil grinned at them like he'd meant to do that.

Or something.

Phil knew engineers. Respected them, but also knew their weak point. *Every single one of them.*

Ask them to do something then convey that maybe you think it is an impossible task, at which point they will move heaven and hell to prove you wrong.

"Let me call a huddle, Phil," Rais said after a few seconds. "I'll call you back."

And the line went dead. About normal for an engineer with an idea.

That was all Phil needed.

Heather grinned at him.

"You're nuts, Phil," she said.

"I am aware of that, *Ground Control*," he retorted, noting the other grins now. "You people didn't think I was going to come all this distance and ***not*** top *CS-405*'s adventures? Oh ye of little faith."

That got more laughs on the line. These were his people. Folks that he had specifically recruited for this mission, or at least interviewed extensively before accepting them.

Warriors, sure, but explorers and rednecks, too. When you got this far from home, there were no right or wrong answers, as long as you tried your damnedest to succeed.

"Is anyone looking frisky or dangerous out there?" Phil asked.

"Negative on all flanks," Leyla replied.

"Secure from action stations but remain on heightened alert," Phil ordered. "Heather, Leyla, and Iveta turn responsibility over to your people and join me aft in person. We need to do some orbital physics, and maybe play a little snooker."

CHAPTER FORTY

Phil looked around the big table at the intent faces staring back. He hadn't told the civilians anything yet, because he didn't know if it would work.

Command Machinist Rais Hosni El-Amin had come forward, but had his entire team on standby aft in case questions came up. It had apparently been a heated debate, as engineers with a bone to chew got. In person, the Command Machinist was a short, kind of pudgy fellow with brown hair graying and brown eyes dark enough that he could have probably transferred to *Aranyani* and fit right in ethnically.

But *Aquitaine* had just about every size, shape, and color ever born on the homeworld, unlike the more homogeneous Balhee Cluster.

"Will it work?" he asked the man simply, causing the room to fall to a silence akin to a tomb.

Rais hemmed a little, his tongue sticking out just a bit.

"We think so," he replied with a wince around his eyes.

Truly impressive, when they usually answered in the bloodthirsty positive.

"Think so?" Phil asked.

"The shield generators are not designed to hold a forward

load like that, for protracted periods, First Centurion," Rais replied. "I've already got a team calculating how we need to adjust things later, but they think it will take two weeks to move pieces around and install extra braces for next time."

"I'm not planning on a next time, El-Amin," Phil retorted.

"Oh, sure, you say that now, Phil, but I know your kind," Rais snarked right back at him, gaining some fire. "A month from now you'll be ready to push a burning dreadnought away from a station the same way and ask me why I haven't fixed it all yet."

That got a round of chuckles, both from the table as well as the projections off other ships, including Kaur Singh and her staff. Command Centurions like him were always asking the engineers for the impossible. Just look at all the crazy things he was known for.

"Risks?" he asked.

"This is where it gets ugly, First Centurion," El-Amin got serious now. "The shields won't just sort of fail if they do. The best estimate is that they would pop like soap bubbles and you'd be driving the nose of the ship into the ground under power before you could do anything to stop it. And none of the corvettes can help, because they don't have nearly the generator power behind them to try a trick like this."

"Remind me to have you design something for pushing burning dreadnoughts," Phil said, getting more laughs. *Aquitaine* tech mixed with *Aditi* and local stuff might come up with something crazy, like a true snowplow he could use to ram a minefield one of these days. "What do we need to do?"

"It will be a balance of shield reinforcement and engine power," El-Amin said. "My folks aft think we can get you into contact, if Leyla can find us a spot stable enough. Iron asteroid ought to be, but we don't know what the interior is."

"I've got four candidates for you, Command Machinist," Leyla spoke up. "Timing on the vector was the key, as every minute we move forward means the asteroid falls that much deeper into the planet's gravity well."

"We need about an hour to completely reconfigure the forward array, from the moment you say go, First Centurion," El-Amin said. "And you'll lose a lot of rear shielding when we do it, as I'm going to be routing them out of the loop. You'll have navigational level, but not much more."

Phil nodded and looked around both the bodies as well as the images on the screen.

"Does anybody have any other possible solutions we should explore?" he asked.

And waited.

Hangdog faces, but most of these people were *Republic of Aquitaine* Navy, and demanded better of themselves. Kaur Singh and her folks thought of themselves as the good guys, as well.

Nobody had anything to offer.

He rapped his knuckles on the table as a way of ending the non-debate.

"All hands move," he said simply. "Rais, you have priority on everybody and any resources needed to get this done. Leyla, you will work with the bridge crew. Iveta, I know you want to handle tactical here, but this won't be combat, so Heather will retain command when we try to push this Sisyphusian rock up the slope of the gravity well. Let's do this, people."

He caught Galia's eye.

"*CC-501*, as we'll be at risk from a combat setting, you will work with *AdCon* Cruiser *Aranyani* to provide layers of defense around us for all of this," he said. "Questions?"

"Negative," she replied. "Anybody sneezes in my direction gets everything we've got."

"And us, as well, First Centurion," Commander Singh added a moment later.

"Thank you," he said to both women.

Screens froze as people locked them at their end. Phil did the same as people rose and raced from the room, leaving him alone with Harinder and her staff.

"What do you think?" he asked her.

"Completely insane," she smiled. "About in line with what I was expecting from you when I signed up for this gig, Phil."

He smiled.

RAN First Centurion Philip S. Kosnett did have a legend to live up to.

CHAPTER FORTY-ONE

Kaur actually stood up and walked over to where she could look at Arya's screens over the woman's shoulder, but that was mostly something to do. Closer to the planet, every vessel that could was hauling people away.

Once Kosnett announced to the system what he was about to try, the possible impact zone shifted, but mostly north, so people were evacuating on an even wider footprint now. That would either work or not, but there was nothing they could do except watch.

It was insane, watching that enormous ship shift delicately into the side of the asteroid like a finger, letting the greater mass of iron begin pushing it backwards and to the side a little. How were they going to do it? *Aranyani* didn't have the gyroscopic power to retain control. And when she'd asked, Leyla had just muttered "Alber' d'Maine" and avoided the question, so Kaur was even deeper in the dark now.

"Status?" she asked Arya.

"They seem confident," the woman replied with a shrug. "I think they are insane, but nothing we've got could even begin to compete with that ship for power or shields."

"How soon?" Kaur pressed.

"Another ten minutes and they think they will be ready to test things, slowly ramping up the engines," her Sub-Commander said. "Oh, hang on. Message coming in. Shit. *Khandoba*."

"I'll take it in my office," Kaur decided.

She didn't know Director Danyal Narang all that well. And he had been aloof towards her the short period he had been here. Had the fleet ordered him to distance himself so she could take any blame that fell?

Possibly, but she'd already known that trouble was coming when that squadron of alien vessels dropped out of jump and hailed them. Everything since then had just reinforced that.

Kaur moved to her day office and settled behind the desk. Apparently, *Aquitaine* commanders spent most of their time here, but Kaur had staff to handle most of the paperwork, and she normally read things in the evening in her cabin, so this space was sparse and a little impersonal.

Her station was on the bridge, regardless of what other Commanders did on their own vessels.

She drew a breath and shifted her face to an innocent visage before flipping the switch to bring the signal live. And the second switch to record everything into her personal log, rather than just ship's communications.

Director Danyal Narang. Half-bald and gray. A bureaucratic Director, rather than a fleet commander. Reputation for being a politician with plans to continue when he went into retirement.

"Director," she nodded gravely.

"I will not pretend that I have the depth of interaction that you have maintained with the visitors, Singh," he began with a hard rumble. "Nor the value. If this fails, your presence as part of their force will compromise the *Aditi Consensus* in the eyes of many systems."

"Will it truly, sir?" she countered. "It appears from where I am sitting that everyone else has already written *Vilahana* off as an inhabited world and is just making sure they are safe from the coming devastation, while Kosnett and his people seem to be the only ones attempting to do anything about that. I would think that we would gain greater reputation for trying."

Kaur did not smile. Nothing to give her superior office a handle. Simple innocence and a fulfillment of her various oaths of service and integrity that were required of a woman intending to take command of a starship.

Narang's face got dark. Not hostile, but less friendly than the little bit it had held before.

"And if I were to order you to withdraw from their side?" he asked.

She noted that he was asking, rather than immediately ordering, so perhaps she had some leeway to make her argument.

"I would find such an order questionable, sir," Kaur said. "The rest of the Cluster will not particularly care, I suspect, but we might burn bridges with a much more sophisticated and advanced society that seems to be asking for our friendship. Do we throw that all away right now?"

Silence. Kaur didn't even move as she watched the impact of her words.

Narang might have sucked a lemon from the look on his face.

Supposedly, he had read the many reports and summaries she had prepared for him, detailing the relationships that she had built with Phil and Heather, as well as many other officers and even a few ambassadors that would be made available. Kaur wondered if Narang understood the honor that Phil and Aliza were doing the *Aditi Consensus* by letting them meet several folks and picking the one they would prefer to deal with, rather than just having an ambassador *assigned*. *Dalou* might get that honor as well, depending on how the Emperor and Shogun reacted, but nobody else.

"Can they even succeed?" he asked, a hint of a sneer in his voice.

"I was present in the meeting when his engineers laid out their thoughts, Director," Kaur replied. "This attempt includes a significant risk that the shields might fail and the ship will slam bow-first into the asteroid while under power. I suspect that the damage would not be catastrophic, but beyond their ability to repair in the field. If nothing else, the arboretum would likely be destroyed if that occurs. That they are still willing to try suggests that they think they can succeed, Director. If they can, then they will have saved *Vilahana* from certain destruction. And we will have stood by their side in their moment of need. Us. The *Aditi Consensus*. No *Gloran* or *Dalou* vessels were asked, nor did they volunteer. First Centurion Kosnett is counting on me to protect his back."

"Why would he need that, if he has all those other vessels?" Narang asked now, confusion emerging onto his brow.

"They will route all shield power forward, sir," she said. "That means hardly anything protecting the rear flanks of the ship if someone were to fire titan bolts or a Power Tap at them. That the corvettes would likely rend someone to death afterwards would not change the fact that *Urumchi* is extremely vulnerable right now."

"Destroyable?" he asked.

Kaur could not hide her gasp. What insanity was this? She studied the man and felt a growl deep in her stomach.

"My job is to crush anyone trying," she said. "Sir."

"And if I ordered you to launch a full attack at *Urumchi* while they were most vulnerable?" he pressed.

Kaur did growl now.

"Ordering me to abandon them would already cause me to question your authority and motives, Director," she said, confident that she had a tape of all this that couldn't just disappear later if powerful agencies got involved.

She might just mail copies of it to every news media on every planet she could find an address for.

"If you were to actually order me to attack our friends at this delicate moment, my crew and I might have to consider a mutiny, ignoring all subsequent orders from you until we could turn ourselves in back at *Aditi* and have this out in public. Sir."

"It will never come out in public, Commander," he growled back. Then his face cleared to the point that a knowing smile emerged. "Nor should it. I wanted to know how committed you were to this rescue, Singh. There are deep tides running right now, and you have been stuck out here where nobody could brief you quietly about things. The arrival of *Aquitaine* has rattled a great many cages. Spies suggest that the *Ingham Syndicate* might be on the verge of civil war. *Dalou* is making ugly noises. The *Gloran Empire* is always looking for a reason to be belligerent. A formal ambassador from *Yaumgan* even arrived at *Aditi*, awaiting Kosnett on the assumption that he would call there next."

"Oh," Kaur said quietly. "Shit."

"Indeed, Kaur," he smiled. "You've gone above and beyond with this mission in more ways than you know, and the Fleet has added another gold star next to your name."

"What are your orders, Director?" she asked, shocked out of her current position by the change in things.

Yaumgan had sent an ambassador to *Aditi* to await Kosnett? ***Yaumgan?***

She could only imagine what their vessel looked like. The philosophers were not constrained by simple things like physics.

"You will find a way to attach yourself to Kosnett's squadron, Commander Singh," Narang said formally. "Since they do not fly a phalanx, you might offer yourself up as a second line, along with the vessel *Viking*, and travel with them. I carry a formal invitation for First Centurion Kosnett to address the Hall of Government on *Aditi*. Hopefully, we can get them next after he saves *Vilahana*."

"You believe he can succeed, Director?" she asked, surprised.

"You believe, Commander," he replied. "That is enough for me."

He cut the line abruptly and Kaur sat there in stunned silence for several minutes.

Yes, she did.

But it would be a thing for the ages to witness.

CHAPTER FORTY-TWO

Heather had taken an extra potty break ahead of time and ordered the wardroom to make the coffee triple strong. Nobody had any idea how long it would take, or if it would even work, but she didn't figure she'd stir from this chair again for many, many hours.

Sergey had been forcibly removed from his forest and was currently being supervised by Phil and Markus on the flag bridge. That way, he wasn't present forward if they lost seals on the arboretum in an emergency and exploded it all to vacuum. She could almost hear his vile mutterings under his breath from here.

Heather glanced once around the room, confirming. She had her First Team present today. Phil had taught her to rotate people around, even putting them on the flag bridge to give them exposure and training, but today she had pulled everyone together.

Iveta sat across from her, wound about as tight as an old-fashioned watch.

Between them was Centurion Bozhidar Virág in his piloting chair, and Centurion Hào Thuần Boyadjiev ready to man the guns. Heather doubted she would be needed, but prepared is prepared.

"Iveta, you and Hào stay alert for anyone causing us trouble, because Leyla will be too focused on the rock to watch our asses hanging out," she said. "That means combat tactical, but let Galia and Kaur handle things unless someone needs Fours to kick his teeth in."

She got quick nods from both of them before opening the intercom aft to the Command Machinist.

"Rais, your folks ready?" she asked as he came up on her small screen.

"Affirmative," he said. "Damage control parties are staged aft of frame seven right now in case we rip her nose off."

"Not coming to that, Command Machinist," Heather growled back at him with a little bit of fire. "Leyla and Bozhidar, confirm your readiness to proceed."

She was back on that moon again, helping Veitengruber steal an imperial police ship by flying pieces around with a crane.

Ground Control. That was why Phil wanted her orchestrating. Things done with meters instead of kilometers, like a flying shuttle having to hold a forward third of a ship exactly to the millimeter while teams poured into the wreckage and set frame bolts as fast as they could.

She thought about Veitengruber and his husband occasionally. Unlike *Stunt Dude*, they had chosen a quiet retirement in *Aquitaine* until such time as they might risk the long journey to *Nov-Lao*, with Deni's knowledge being put to use teaching people here about the far side of the galaxy and what they might find beyond the former *Holding of Man.*

Dead gods and good riddance.

"All sensors locked in," Leyla said. "Almost a seismographic level of detail, but I'm filtering most of it out as this should be one cold ball of iron. We are currently holding station exactly on line and in parallel with the planetary surface, Commander."

Heather nodded.

It was time.

"*Ground Control* to flag bridge," she said, keying Phil. "*RAN Urumchi* is in readiness."

Phil studied her for a long second, as if he could see the transformation she could feel already happening under her skin. *Lady Blackbeard* had required her to jump across open space at a fleeing starship in the middle of a hostile star system, which had been the craziest thing Heather could ever remember doing to that point.

To that point.

Before *Ground Control.*

"*Ground Control,* you have the flag," Phil said simply.

"I have the flag," Heather replied automatically.

Most of her was back in the *Mansi* system that first time. *Mansi-D,* the gas giant out on the edge of the warm zones. Third moon, where *Buran* had left a boneyard of small fighters and patrol cutters they had captured from *Fribourg* during the long war.

After depositing the senior officers on *Mansi-B* to live out the rest of their lives.

Ground Control.

"Pilot, engage forward thrusters one percent," she called out. "Target is strike zone alpha."

"One percent forward," Bozhidar replied evenly. "Alpha coming up."

"All hands, brace for collision," Heather said.

Nobody knew what the hell would happen when the big lady tried to shove a rock out of the way with her forward shield array. Hopefully one percent would be enough to ripple everyone else's coffee. Hers was in a sippy cup with the lid sealed tight for that reason. Someone would refill it when she wasn't looking.

Heather was already vibrating with mad energy. This might not top the rescue on *Mansi,* but damned if it wouldn't be close at the end of the day.

"Twenty meters," Leyla called the range. "Ten. Contact."

Something passed through the entire keel longways.

Heather had been in a petite earthquake when she was young, like the wake of a boat passing under her from behind and then leaving. Barely a three on the Richter Scale, and that shallow. She'd only been a few kilometers from the epicenter, but it had been enough for her to shiver then.

"Pilot, stabilize yourself on the gyros before we proceed."

Ground Control was talking now, not Command Centurion Heather Lau. *Mansi-D-3*, all over again, but instead of a crane she had a bulldozer named *Urumchi*.

The margin of error hadn't gotten any wider in the years since.

"Ship stable on gyros, Commander," Bozhidar replied after a few seconds.

"*Aquitaine* squadron, this is *Ground Control*, I have the flag," she said calmly over the wide channel, unable to call herself anything else right now. "Stand by for a miracle."

Green lights, even from the *Aditi* folks, but she was including them as *RAN* today. Everyone else was safely beyond the range of risk, while *Aranyani* had chosen to stand with them.

With her.

"Pilot, bring your power up to seven percent and hold there," *Ground Control* spoke from her mouth like an ancient oracle possessed by a goddess.

Urumchi shivered as though it had cold flesh around her.

"Seven percent achieved," the pilot in front of her called calmly. Bozhidar did everything calmly. That's why he was flying today. "Verticality is stable."

"*CM-507*, call the deflection," she called out now. *RAN Viking* would have done it, but they were all having adventures somewhere and missing all the fun. Barnaby would never let her hear the end of it when he got back.

"Negative deflection, *Ground Control*," Isabèl replied quickly.

She would allow everyone that privilege today, to call her by that *other* name. Even if there was a burning dreadnought in her future, this would be the first time anyone had ever tried something this insane. Hope to all the gods listening it was the last.

She listened to the ship around her. They were never silent beasts, even if all the chimes and beeps are turned off, because the hull flexes and twists with differential heating, both outside and in.

Urumchi spoke to her like a goddess, whispering to her of the gray lady's readiness.

"Pilot, come up to eleven percent on forward thrusters and hold," *Ground Control* said. "Sensors, measure surface deformation caused by the forward shields."

She couldn't even explain to herself why it mattered, but it did.

"The ground is compressing ahead of us," Leyla replied. "Four meters and holding."

Two and a half Heather's tall. She could work with that.

"Engineering, what shield deformation do you measure?" she asked.

Rais had expected almost none. They would work or they would fail. Simple as that.

"Marginal, Flag," he replied instantly, but that was the only thing he had to do until something else happened.

Like now.

"Engineering, stand by for main engines," *Ground Control* ordered.

She paused and drew a breath, listening now like she had then. Harmonics of stress changing as everything about her settled into new forms.

Her, Veitengruber, and a dead starship they were intent on stealing from the surface of a dead moon.

Painted with the flag of the *Seventeenth Imperial Police*

Protectorate. Because those had been the poor souls overwhelmed by a shark striking from the hidden depths.

Nobody screamed a warning. She wasn't even sure they were breathing, or if she had entered a dreamworld where everyone around her had been turned to alabaster.

"Pilot, ahead one quarter power," she said aloud, shattering the chains that held that man in stasis.

"Ahead one quarter, aye," came the reply.

So automatic you didn't think about it, because that sort of thing happened almost daily for years. Decades at this point.

Urumchi quivered with power, but her song did not change.

Everyone else held their breath, but they'd never done this before.

Ground Control.

"Ahead two-thirds power," she called now, letting those monstrous workhorses run.

"Two-thirds, aye."

"*CM-507?*"

"We are showing a minor deflection, Flag. Nothing sufficient, but measurable."

She nodded.

"Pilot, bring everything slowly to ninety-three percent."

"Ninety-three percent, aye."

Urumchi's quiver turned into a vibration that would have everyone grasping at their coffee before they spilled. Around her, gasps as they felt it, finally traveling to that place Heather had been for the last hour.

Mansi-D-3.

"Engineering, I want all reactors and engines pushed into the redline and held there," *Ground Control* announced.

"For how long, Flag?" Rais asked.

"Until I order otherwise."

"Stand by."

At least those rednecks aft had been prepared for such an

order. The tone in her breastbone went up a minor third over the course of thirty seconds.

"Engineering, how long until something breaks aft?"

"Your guess is probably better than mine, *Ground Control.*"

She nodded. It probably was. This was her ship. Her body. The rest just crewed it for her.

"Pilot, route an extra bit of juice to the aft gyroscopes."

Bozhidar actually looked up at her, blinking with the whites of eyes visible. She harpooned the man with her will and he nodded blankly.

"Aft gyroscopes, aye."

Ground Control smiled.

It would hold. Long enough.

Even if she ended up breaking the ship in the process, *Urumchi* would hold.

CHAPTER FORTY-THREE

That, to Phil, was still the downside of being First Centurion. That fifth stripe meant everyone was subordinate, but it also meant that he no longer *did* things.

Phil Kosnett ordered, and others made things happen.

Because he had been given the resources by Pet, he had the right people. Three years of late nights in her office with stacks of personnel files to wade through guaranteed that.

He had never heard a starship make noises like his flagship, but then, he was attempting to top the fabled *Rescue at Mansi* today, at least in the legends that would accrue starting tomorrow.

"Encrypted text message from the *Aditi* Ship of the line *Khandoba*," Harinder said quietly. "Using a key *Aranyani* previously shared with us."

Around them, a rock was moving slowly out of the path of slamming into a planet in another ten hours or so, pushed sideways by *Urumchi.*

Phil nodded to the woman and she sent it to his screen.

Secretly monitoring pirate traffic, it read. *Kaur Singh has shared suggestions* Ingham *behind attack on* Vilahana. *They are preparing to run. Should we engage?*

Well, wasn't *that* interesting?

Kaur had suggested that the Director sent from home might be more ambivalent about things. Certainly, the man had approached the last few days with a jaundiced eye, at least in the small amount of interactions that Phil had had before tomorrow's event.

Today's event. It was the middle of the night down on *Vilahana*. The sun would be rising soon down there.

Hopefully, not to have a second sun join it and sear the planetary surface like had happened to *St. Legier*. Phil had been to the aftermath, to see places where the ground itself had been melted like glass and then left as a reminder to future generations.

If it was indeed *Ingham*, they had chosen the stupidest possible way in the galaxy to get on Phil's bad side. He would move heaven and hell to get them all.

Even hell wouldn't be safe for them. Not from his wrath.

He typed slowly, forming his thoughts as he wanted them read back to him at his later court martial. There were always Court Martials for big things, and they weren't necessarily bad. The *RAN* wanted to publicly review actions taken by Command Centurions and higher, to make sure that good decisions were transmitted to the fleet as much as bad things.

It helped draw that bright line over which younger officers needed to occasionally stride.

Rescuing *Vilahana* would not generate the need for a Court. Asking an *Aditi* Ship of the Line to have a go at some pirates without concrete proof, however…

But it also put the *Aditi Consensus* firmly on his side after this. They would be making a public statement that the galaxy had changed. That old things might no longer be allowed to slide.

Being denied trade permission at an *Aditi* world would no longer be considered a sufficient punishment, if armed squadrons began hunting down your ships and capturing or destroying them instead.

He wanted to let this one go. He really did.

But in his heart, Phil knew that anyone willing to bombard an inhabited world wasn't playing nice anymore. That his mere presence in the Balhee Cluster had caused a significant rupture in their entire shared culture.

He was suddenly standing on that same precipice that Jessica Keller had talked to him about after the *Horvat Incident*. And Arlo nearly killing him. Contemplating *Thuringwell*, when she had managed to convince Karl VII to sue for peace and mean it this time.

And then later. Everything that had happened at the wedding she had been invited to attend. The one where Karl VII made Arlo an Imperial Ritter and Honorary Colonel of an Imperial Division. Where he had turned Moirrey Kermode into a legend.

When a coup had nearly turned into a revolution, but for Jessica Keller and Casey Weigand standing in the middle of the road and saying simply, "No, you move."

Phil typed the words and reviewed them several times. He even crooked a finger at Harinder to walk around to his side of the table and read the entire exchange before he transmitted it.

She made one minor tweak in his language, but he found her wording better and kept it.

Offer accepted. Stand by for hunters to flush your game.

Phil hit transmit as Harinder returned to her seat.

"*Aquitaine* squadron, this is Kosnett," he said in a tone that wouldn't sound too bad when the Judge Advocate General played it back to the court later. "I have the squadron flag while *Ground Control* maintains her operation. *Task Force 502*, form up in phalanx ahead of *AdCon* Cruiser *Aranyani*, and prepare to engage hostile forces. *Aranyani*, come about to heading One-One-Five and accelerate to attack speed."

Phil felt the entire gravitational pull of the Balhee Cluster shift as he spoke. Around him, the various Yeoman, Chiefs, and Centurions that made up his Flag Staff gave off a collective sound that was only a gasp when amplified by twenty mouths.

There was a new sheriff in town. One with a lot less ambivalence to the sorts of shit you people used to get away with.

Phil leaned back and watched the future begin to unfold.

CHAPTER FORTY-FOUR

Kaur gasped along with the others when Phil gave her the order. She was on a squadron circuit with all of the *Aquitaine* vessels, but that was merely to make it easier for her to communicate with them.

One-One-Five happened to point her bow almost directly at *Tango* and his two escorts. *Aranyani* was superior to any one of them, with *Tango* being only a little lighter overall than her cruiser, but adding a Raider and a Picket on his side gave him a significant edge in a duel.

Task Force 502, however, could probably take the three of them *without* her help.

"Jagadish, bring us to the new heading and engage," Kaur said, echoing Phil's order. "Nam, charge everything and prepare to use it. Give me long-range warheads on the titan bolts and use them as soon as we get into range, then go for short range and overload them as much as you can."

"Affirmative, Commander," Nam replied. "What about *Atlas* and *Maddog*?"

"We know that Utkin sent home a pair of Raiders loaded with missile racks," Kaur replied. "So I presume titan bolts or maybe firebirds, like *Tango* has. Let the escorts handle it, but tell them what a firebird is and how to fight it. No, let me. You prepare for combat."

"Roger that."

Aquitaine Command Centurion Erle Kuiper was on line, looking at her expectantly. Her three ships were already forming up, but those corvettes had a much higher power/mass curve, so they could out-accelerate her.

"You have seen the titan bolt, Command Centurion," Kaur said, waiting for the woman to nod. "The *Dalou Hegemony* has invented a variant they call a firebird. It moves slower than a titan bolt, about as fast as many missiles when they have reached peak acceleration, but it cannot be destroyed as easily, because the weapon, at its heart, is a magnetically-contained ball of plasma. They come in four sizes, with the largest rare on anything less than a *Dalou* battleship."

"How *do* we kill it?" Erle asked.

"Like you would a missile swarm," Kaur replied. "Hit it with your Pulse-Two several times, knocking plasma loose from the core as it closes. If you hit it hard enough, enough times, it might more or less evaporate. *Aranyani* does not have sufficient guns of either size to do that, which is why I presume Phil sent you with us."

"Understood, Commander," Erle said. "I'll bring *504* and *506* in tighter and we'll fly in a shield line rank ahead of you."

"Coordinate that with Jagadish Misra directly," Kaur said. "We'll stay bow-on to *Tango* until he surrenders or more likely flees us."

"Engaging now."

Kaur sat back and smiled at Misra when he glanced at her. If *Tango* stood to fight, that ship would likely be annihilated, so she expected a full-speed retreat. She could not think of a better way to train a young officer than to have him in charge at a time when it might not be life and death here.

Task Force 502 gave her that option.
She owed the *Ingham Syndicate*. Time to deliver the bill.
And collect it.

241

Ground Control heard the change before it even registered on a gauge somewhere aft. Something had gone wrong. Or was about to.

"Pilot! All engines cut to zero!" she yelled over the already-quiet bridge. "Now! Extra power to the forward shield array."

Centurion Virág was on autopilot at this moment, not even thinking as he had merely become an extension of her will. His hands danced across the board as fast as she spoke the words.

Urumchi changed pitch. The vibration became a low hum, down nearly an octave.

"Engineering, damage control status," she called over the line. "Pilot, maintain heading and keep us in contact with thrusters alone."

"Aye."

"How did you know?" Rais asked, a hint of fear and wonder in his voice. "We nearly lost array six with some sort of local overload. Probably would have cascaded if it did."

She couldn't explain it to the man, any more than she could have described blue to someone born without eyes. But she was only marginally present on the bridge of her ship. Much of her was back on *Mansi-D-3*, holding everything in place on harmonics alone as Veitengruber slid the forward section of his new ship into place with nothing but fingertips to hold it.

The song had changed.

"How long to repair?" she asked.

"Didn't break, *Ground Control*," Rais replied, shifting to technical voice now. "We need to adjust a few settings and maybe swap out some breakers that might have just used up most of their effective lifespan in an hour instead of a month. Give me four minutes and I'll know."

She nodded, still feeling like an oracle possessed by a benevolent goddess. One that didn't want *Urumchi* dead. Or maybe *Vilahana* had a guardian spirit who had welcomed their help today.

Ground Control looked around the bridge at the awe and surprise she saw staring back at her. Another person might have made a joke right now. Laughed it off.

She was too far into a zone to do that.

Phil caught her eye on her screen.

"Seventeenth Imperial Police Protectorate," he said simply. Not even a question.

She nodded. Markus and *Stunt Dude* were the only others present that would truly understand what that meant.

Phil nodded and smiled at her.

"You got them home safe, too, you know," he reminded her.

She had. Stage managed the entire performance that resulted in *RAN Persephone* joining the fleet for a short period of time. Just long enough to launch a full frontal assault on the guard station over *Mansi-B*, coming out of jump at high speed and surprising those heartless pricks.

And then shattering them to liberate the planet below.

"*CM-507*, what is our glide path?" she spoke aloud now.

Just another day at the office for the *Republic of Aquitaine* Navy.

"Insufficient, *Ground Control*," Isabèl replied. "Significant, but you are not clear of the planet."

She nodded. Again, *Ground Control* could not explain how she knew that. Or that she knew exactly how much more of a push was needed.

She brought up the orbital geometry on her screen and echoed it against the things in her head.

Yes.

"Pilot, reverse thrusters ten percent and back us away from the surface," she ordered. "Sensors, guide him around to strike point gamma."

Gasps, but hands moved.

She could stay right here and keep pushing. But moving to gamma right now would let her push the rock up and over to the point that it fell entirely out of the gravitational pull of *Vilahana*. Nobody would be able to secretly use a Pressor Beam and sneak it up on the planet ever again when she was done, as it would move into a cometary orbit instead.

They could deal with it from there. Rais and his Shield Projector tugboat could push it someplace safe. Or use it for target practice and break it into rubble that would burn up instead of impacting or exploding.

Tomorrow.

Rais returned.

"We're ready, *Ground Control*," he said simply, those words summing up what was probably a vast Bollywood of activity aft as all of his people moved in harmony to fix the ship.

"Strike point gamma coming up," Bozhidar called out. "Approaching at one percent thruster power now."

She watched as they closed.

"All hands, brace for collision."

Contact.

Again, that shiver running down the entire length of the hull like a wake.

"We have made contact with gamma."

"Stabilize on gyros," she ordered. "Increase aft power twenty-five percent."

Possibly shaved a year off of their operational life doing this, but she suspected that *Urumchi* would need a drydock sooner rather than later anyway, just to confirm that she hadn't bent anything with this stunt. Maybe at *Aditi*, depending on how Phil was received. The technology would flood the cluster eventually anyway. Might as well start with friends.

"Pilot, are you ready?"

"Affirmative."

"Main engines ahead one quarter."

The surge of power and song returned.

"Engineering, are we stable?" she asked, turning her terrible gaze to Rais El-Amin on the screen.

He was looking down at something else.

"Up a little more," Rais yelled at someone off screen. Someone replied with a sound that was little more than a grunt on the pickup.

"You should be good now," he said, looking up at her. His dark eyes were deadly serious, but they'd all gone to a different place than they'd been in just a few hours ago.

"Pilot, slowly bring the main engines to ninety-eight percent," she ordered.

Again the quiver. The harmonics of the hull and forward shield array taking a load they were never intended to bear. *Atlas*, holding up the world, unlike that pipsqueak pirate across the way just watching right now.

At least until Phil's surprise registered on them.

She and *Urumchi* had a task right now.

They could hunt later.

CHAPTER FORTY-SIX

INGHAM ENFORCER TANGO

"What?" Basant demanded. "Repeat that!"

"*Aranyani* and three of the escorts just broke orbit of the asteroid, Commander," Mati said again. "They are currently pointed this direction and accelerating."

Damn it!

"Bring up the projection," he ordered.

The rock was still out a ways, closing at a deceptively-rapid pace, but already it was clear that the strangers had done the impossible. They had actually used a battleship as a tugboat to push a rock that massive off-line. It was just a matter of time until the scanner shifted to green.

That bitch in the *Aditi* cruiser was charging this way, with a phalanx in front of her. *Saluki* was functionally abandoned, but he'd been aboard to see what those ships had done to it the first time. They couldn't even run this time, but the only people left aboard right now were engineers who didn't have any outstanding warrants on an *Aditi* world, just in case they were boarded and arrested.

"What will they be able to do to our firebirds?" Basant asked now.

"No clue, Commander," Mati replied. "They have rapid-firing beams, and I presume *Aditi* will warn them. Worth finding out?"

Basant studied the tactical arrangement. His firebird mount on the bow was a crane, the second heaviest weapon possible, behind only the condor, with a pair of falcons, one over each engine pylon. *Atlas* had three falcons. *Maddog* had a pair of titan bolts that wouldn't matter much, other than they might hit and soften up one of those impossible shield facings for the firebird to hit.

The enemy was above him in the overall gravity well, but charging sideways now across the plane, so he could always withdraw. Everyone else had stayed well clear of the zone that *Aquitaine* had declared, so that worked against the newcomers now.

He had time.

"Let them charge," Basant ordered. "All ships turn to Zero-Three-Five and begin accelerating. Prepare to come about on gyroscopes to a heading of Three-Four-Zero and go for maximum speed, but only after they commit. We'll run down their flank while we stay back from those shorter range aft guns. *Maddog*, standard warheads on your titan bolts. Everyone else load firebirds and stand by with them in the tubes."

It was not a fair fight, by any stretch of the imagination. *Tango* was not the equal of *Aranyani*. *Atlas* and *Maddog* were nowhere close to matching three escorts. He would have to run.

Worse, he had failed. The Directorate would probably hang him out to dry and throw him and Andrea to the wolves in an attempt to buy peace with *Aditi*. Might even announce that they were going to go straight.

Even *Aditi* wasn't dumb enough to fall for that, but it would confuse things. Buy Basant time. Other commanders would be unwilling to offer themselves up to the law. Too many of them were facing decades or lifetimes inside boxes, assuming that *Aquitaine* didn't demand that they be executed.

Ingham might be done. But *Hamath, Gilas, Wisym,* and the others would be in no better shape.

Zen-Mekyo civil war? There were a lot of unclaimed worlds in the *Dalou* neutral zone. Good places to hide. Maybe build up new bases to raid from, because the Directorate would probably try to buy amnesty by selling all the current maps.

Damn them!

"Enemy squadron is closing now," Mati called, breaking through Basant's rage.

"Come to Zero-Three-Five and accelerate," he ordered all three ships. "Prepare to open fire."

"I have movement on our flank," Mati suddenly yelled. "Oh, shit! That battleship just locked targeting arrays on us!"

"Spin the Shield Projector to cover him," Basant countered. "Now! Turn on your gyros and go for maximum speed now. All ships target the escort in the center of the front line and fire as you have an arc. Forget fighting. Run for the edge of the gravity well. We'll meet up again at Kyunku Point as quickly as everyone can get there."

"Power tap coming on-line, Commander," Mati yelled. "And a second one."

"Evasive maneuvering," Basant ordered.

He was facing three power taps, as well as six titan bolts, if he stayed put. Enough to crush him. Maybe take the three of them down, without *Aranyani.*

He had to escape. Warn Andrea and the other ships that their days of lazy piracy were over.

And maybe start a war.

CHAPTER FORTY-SEVEN

ADCON CRUISER ARANYANI

Kaur watched the screen and studied the bow of *Tango* as the sensors tried to read intent. She'd fought him only the once, but pirates were not trained in combat maneuvering.

"*Khandoba* just locked on *Tango*," Arya said in a loud-enough voice. "Expect maneuvering."

Yes. He could not stand before a Ship of the Line, even with help. Less so with her closing the other arm of the pincer trap on him. *Tango* had one way to go right now, if he wanted to survive the day.

"Squadron come right thirty degrees and accelerate," she ordered.

Erle Kuiper gave her a surprised look, but Kaur supposed that *Aquitaine* would have gone straight for the throat right now.

"*Tango* just put out a firebird," Arya called. "Falcon type. Launch jammers?"

Jammers. Standard procedure when facing firebirds was to start coasting immediately. Turn off all your sensors and scanners so it might mistake you for a large rock. Launch a small missile designed to mimic the original sensor image of *Aranyani* to the primitive systems guiding a firebird.

Useful way to keep from getting hammered by the *Dalou*, but you sacrificed control of the battle in trade for not getting beaten down into the mud. *Tango* would get away.

"Negative on jammers," Kaur decided. "*Task Force 502*, expect several more like it, so engage slowly."

"*CB-502*, that firebird is tracking you, not *Aranyani*," Arya called out. "Go evasive."

"Negative on evasive, Squadron Flag," Erle called back almost laconically. "Stand by."

Atlas launched a pair of falcons now. Arya would be updating their records for future encounters. *Tango* launched another falcon and then put a crane onto the field. *Atlas* sent off their third and last falcon. *Maddog's* twin titan bolts were almost an afterthought.

"Nam, hit the crane with Main Guns and Point Guns both," Kaur ordered. "Lock the power tap and titan bolts on *Tango* and fire at will. Reload as fast as you can and maintain that firing split until something changes."

"Roger that, Commander," Nam called back over her shoulder.

Kaur had only rarely seen this much firepower on a battlefield, not counting training exercises. *Tango* and his mates were going for broke.

But so were Erle and her two commanders.

CG-504 and *CG-506* suddenly slid even closer to *CB-502*. *502* slowed down and now the three ships formed a triangle with the tip pointed backwards at *Aranyani*. The ships drifted their bows to the right, tracking on *Tango's* flight path, but more importantly bringing their aft battery to bear.

The scorpion.

Kaur had been too focused on staying alive the last time to watch this task force really work, although she had reviewed the tapes several times with her officers. But that had been attacking.

Task Force 502 was designed to escort *Urumchi* and *Viking* in the event of a battle.

Type-3-Pulse beams and Pulse-Two fire licked out individually as she watched, when Kaur had been expecting all of them to rapid fire. What were they doing?

Oh.

Erle Kuiper was watching her scanners as each bolt hit, and calibrating what the effect was. New weapon for them, they would want to know the best way to kill it.

Kaur Singh had no doubt that they would be intent on killing things like that. Those crews gave off that aura.

Her own Main Guns and Point Guns were part of the sequence, but only a small part. Kaur watched the power tap begin hammering *Tango's* flank shielding. He'd left his Shield Projector the other direction, as *Khandoba* was also raining hell on him, from closer and with more weapons.

One of the titan bolts scored metal.

"Excellent shooting, Nam," Kaur called.

Long range, target in full evasion and madly accelerating, without even bothering to fire anything back over a shoulder at her.

Maddog was the fastest. It hit the edge of safety first and vanished. Maybe even a little too soon, but perhaps that commander just wanted to get several light hours away so they could be safe now and fix everything later.

Atlas and *Tango* seemed to be in a dead heat race. Whether that was for first place or last was hard to tell, but *Tango* was suffering damage as shots got through collapsed shields and cut steel.

Wouldn't be enough to stop him, but nothing short of his destruction probably would be at this point.

And he had fired first. Let the records show that *Aranyani* was defending herself against *Zen-Mekyo* aggression.

Never forget the court of public opinion, especially if *Ingham* had tried to destroy an inhabited world.

Kaur turned back to the firebirds as *Tango* got too far away to hit. The crane was shedding plasma hard under the withering fire. Of the five firebirds, two appeared to have been reduced to ghosts, which was impressive.

That left three more firebirds tracking the leader.

Kaur held her breath as the three ships switched now to rapid fire, pouring everything they had into the various bolts, even as *Khandoba* fired a few Main Gun shots at extreme range to try to help.

If they were sailing on water, Kaur would have said that a fog had just arisen, from the way plasma clouds streamed out. She almost expected that the various firebirds had turned into comets, with tails pointed out behind them on a clear, fall night.

Impact.

The leader vanished inside a flash of light so bright that her scanners automatically dimmed it.

"*CB-502*, what is your status?" she yelled over the comm.

Her signal had gone heavy with static.

"Slightly sunburned, but intact," Kuiper replied after a few seconds. "Forward shields held."

Held? Under that load?

Kaur muted the line and turned to Arya.

"Make sure all of us review the sensor logs of impact," she ordered. "I want to know what just happened, and compare it to the story Kosnett will tell the rest of the cluster."

Arya nodded.

"Message from *Tango*," Arya perked up.

"Main screen."

Basant Utkin. Tall, dark, and probably handsome if you were into barroom brawlers with broken noses. Kaur had known a few fellow officers like that.

"We're not done, *Aranyani*," he said simply, and then the message ended.

"Reply?" Arya asked.

"No," Kaur decided. "Let him have the last word today. I'm pretty sure Phil will have something better to say, when this is all said and done. Any other enemy vessels?"

"Negative," Arya replied. "*Tango* and *Atlas* just jumped."

"Secure from combat and prepare to return to assist *Urumchi*," Kaur said. "Compliments to *Khandoba* for their assistance, while you are at it."

"And then?" Nam asked.

"And then maybe we can finally go home."

EPILOGUES

CHAPTER 48

DATE OF THE REPUBLIC MAY 2, 411 RAN URUMCHI,
VILAHANA ORBIT

Ground Control felt it in her bones. Right at the center of her breastbone, her own keel vibrating in harmony with *Urumchi*'s. They had cleared the gravity deflection that *Vilahana* had started to induce. The rock would fall past the planet, slingshot down and across, and quickly head out into deep space now.

Not even remaining in close orbit, but racing out into the darkness, where it would become hopefully nothing more than a navigational hazard and a trivia answer to future travelers.

"*CM-507*, confirm the deflection," *Ground Control* said as the bridge crew around her started to cheer and whistle.

She dialed up the sound on the main comm, just so it would be audible.

"Confirmed, *Ground Control*," Isabèl replied. "Asteroid will remain high enough to pass safely over the north pole of the planet on the way out again."

Heather nodded and relaxed.

Six hours to spare, but she'd known for the last hour that they would succeed. Just couldn't speak those words aloud until the goddess released her from that geas.

She flexed a stiff back and pulled both of her shoulder blades together with a pop, then rotated her head left and right and stretched her jaw.

A shower was also in order, just from the funk she was emitting right now. Most of them probably needed showers. Maybe naps.

She'd been going for about twenty-four hours straight at this point, all of it out at the sharp end of the spear.

"Pilot, shut down main engines and prepare to reverse thrusters," Heather called, finally causing some of the bedlam around her to subside.

They were all still on duty, partying or not. She planned to get a little drunk later with dinner, just so she'd be able to sleep eventually.

"Standing by!" Bozhidar yelled, further startling people.

He never yelled. Faces turned shocked and sober in reaction. He also grinned at her, so he was aware of what would happen.

"Reverse course One-Eight-Zero," Heather ordered. "Get us clear then bring everything to a full stop, preparatory to a normal orbital insertion."

Heather took one more deep breath and pondered if she should get a tattoo of that shield logo of the *Seventeenth Imperial Police Protectorate* on the back of her shoulder. Or maybe her bottom. Someplace almost nobody would ever see it, but to remind her. Maybe add a bar for *Vilahana* underneath it, so she could add a second one when Rais was right and Phil had her do this again, one of these days.

She'd worry about that later.

Phil was waiting on the screen.

"Flag Bridge, this is Heather Lau, aboard *Urumchi*," the words tumbled out automatically. "Mission is successful."

If something that simple could sum up everything that had just occurred. Maybe. Maybe she needed a tattoo, after all.

"I have the flag," Phil said, just as simply.

Heather felt the weight of *Ground Control* slide off her shoulders.

"The *Ingham* squadron has fled under fire," Phil continued. "We are working with Director Narang on the *Aditi Consensus* Ship of the Line *Khandoba* to let everyone know how this happened and what we did to stop it."

Heather supposed that she'd probably missed a lot over the last several hours, but she'd only been on the bridge of *Urumchi* physically. Mentally and emotionally she had been elsewhere.

Maybe inside a mountain in northern Greece, back before *Earth* was destroyed so long ago. At Delphi.

Maybe just *Mansi-D-3*.

The logs and tapes could be skimmed tomorrow. Or she could corner Harinder over dinner and get the executive summary. Something.

"What are your orders, First Centurion?" she asked.

"Return to *Vilahana*," he told her. "I'll go back aboard *Aranyani* for the flight down. You will join me, Heather, with Iveta in command here. There are going to be a lot of people who would like to thank you personally."

Yes, she supposed there would be.

The Governor might even have a better booze selection than the aft crew lounge.

Maybe, just maybe, someone around there would know a good tattoo artist.

CHAPTER 49
ADCON CRUISER ARANYANI

Kaur would not have believed it, had she not been present watching. Too much like a lurid science fiction story, but *Urumchi* and Kosnett had done it. Had actually pushed an asteroid with nothing more than their forward shield array. Not even a Shield Projector.

If anything was going to bring home to the rest of the cluster the technological edge *Aquitaine* had over everyone else, that was it. Hopefully the wiser heads would prevail over any fools seeing Phil Kosnett as a conqueror coming for them.

"Jagadish, what is our status?" she asked.

"First Centurion's shuttle is preparing to dock now, Commander," he replied.

"You have the bridge, Misra," she said. "Arya and Nam with me."

They rose and headed aft, where they could greet the man.

Phil didn't need to return to the planetary surface aboard her boom. He had shuttles and even those heavier craft the crew had referred to as gunboats. Somewhere less than a frigate, but still heavily armed with a Pulse-Two on the bow.

That he was coming aboard was a statement of purpose from the man. Letting everyone know that he saw the *Aditi Consensus* as an ally and a friend. The rest of the nations of the Cluster could draw their own lessons from that. Hopefully, they would be good ones.

She led the other two women back down the main corridor and over the threshold to the secondary hull. With the booms detached, everyone needed the ability to get little shuttles back and forth, although *Aranyani* carried only three administrative shuttles, none of which could haul much cargo.

You didn't need more, when the boom itself could land.

She wondered if *Aquitaine* would build something similar, one of these days, or if they had already moved beyond such things, as they had with so many other avenues.

The bay was open to space beyond the window as the shuttle approached. Kaur watched it enter and then drift delicately closer before spinning in place as the door closed. Lights came on and blinked as everything closed up and Kaur found herself wondering at the future that awaited them on the planetary surface.

The conference had been delayed two days to give everyone a chance to recover from everything that had happened. People had to return to homes and businesses they had madly fled in the face of catastrophe. The whole planet had blinked, and now needed to reset.

She supposed that all eyes would return to the conference, and that gave everyone an external focus. That would be good.

They would never return to normalcy. Kaur was certain that any number of future pathways had been eliminated over the last week. But the remaining ones were brighter than they had been.

She smiled as the hatch on the shuttle opened and Harinder Abbatelli emerged first. Not even with the usual combat teams, because Phil had instructed them to meet him on the surface in their own craft.

Aliza Babatunde came next, falling into line next to Harinder, both of them in their day uniforms with three and four white stripes on the right arm. Phil was next, which did surprise her. Hadn't Heather come with them?

But then he fell into line next to Aliza and Kaur understood. He was honoring the woman who had truly saved the day. Everyone else had helped, but the one known as *Ground Control* had held the weight of the entire Cluster on her own shoulders.

She stepped out and Kaur noted the snort and eye roll as she caught sight of Phil standing there.

The inner airlock was finally open, so Kaur led Nam and Arya into the bay to greet them.

It looked a little odd to Kaur as she counted noses. Phil was the only male officer present, not counting flight engineers moving about. Three females from *Aquitaine*, all Command Centurions or Fleet Centurion. Her and her top two officers.

Phil had said that *Fribourg* had been entirely male in their naval forces, even now, although the first generation of young women was being allowed to enlist and attend their various naval schools, under the stern, watchful gaze of the first female Emperor ever.

Kaur made a note to visit *Fribourg* one of these days, just to see what all that meant.

"Greetings and welcome," she said as she came to a stop, directly in front of Heather, Phil to her immediate left.

"Thank you," Heather said.

They exchanged salutes, because you were supposed to do that with visiting officers, but it broke into informality quickly. Arya tended to hug, and captured Heather before the woman could escape.

Even Phil allowed himself a new level of informality, but they had all done the impossible.

Quickly, though, Kaur got them rounded up and moving forward.

"Heather, you take my seat," Kaur said. "I'll join Phil, Harinder, and Aliza."

The woman looked dubious, but Kaur knew that she had

never been one for the limelight. Quiet and professional, in spite of the things Phil and the others had mentioned or whispered about his amazing Command Centurion.

Heather looked at her blankly, but Kaur just smiled.

"You give the order," she said simply.

It was instructional, watching Heather Lau square her shoulders and thrust her jaw forward, as if calling on all that hidden, inner strength now.

"I have the flag," Heather said simply, but everyone understood now what that meant, spoken between *Aquitaine* officers. "Pilot, detach the *Energiya Module*."

Harinder, of all people, had been the one to explain the most about *Buran*, that immortal, electronic god that had plagued the far, inner portions of the galactic arm where *Fribourg* and *Aquitaine* lived. The *Sentient* warships who enforced the will of a god on a population that had no freedom at all.

Phil and Heather had grown famous in their own portion of that war, although the terrible demigoddess Jessica Keller was the one that invoked the most dread and awe here in the Balhee Cluster.

Jagadish hesitated, but only for a fraction before he translated the words and began typing in commands. Around them, the central pylon began to unlock with sounds like a church playing off-tune bells to summon the faithful.

Fortunately, Jagadish didn't wait for the full suite of orders Kaur normally gave, but went ahead and initiated the forward thrusters to push them into open space like a sword emerging from its scabbard.

Time passed in silence, save for the sounds of various systems notifying people of status.

"Module detached, Commander," Jagadish turned back to Heather and smiled.

She nodded, still too serious for Kaur's sake, but maybe she felt like she was on stage again? The woman had always struck Kaur as something of an introvert, so that made sense.

"Engines ahead for deorbital glide, Pilot," Heather continued.

Jagadish nodded and went back to work.

Close enough, and Kaur had an excellent crew. They all wanted to show off for Heather a little, today.

Kaur watched everyone settle some as the boom began to turn and slowly dive towards the atmosphere. Overhead, the entire *Aquitaine* squadron, minus only *Viking*, was at a combat alert similar to the escape three days ago, but Kaur didn't expect anyone would misbehave today.

Tomorrow would take care of itself.

CHAPTER 50

Phil noted the way the formal guards perked up as the ground transport deposited him at the front entrance. Heads turned and whispers broke out, rippling back into the building quickly.

Three days ago, this was going to be a semi-formal event where all the various players in the region could stand around and make trade deals. Lubricate commerce, because Pet had drawn the correct lessons from Jessica Keller and Casey Weigand. Even initially mismatched trade causes hostilities to break down over time, as more and more people found that they can get rich faster and more reliably from trade than from plunder.

Or piracy.

He still expected to crack a few heads together before this was all done, but that was fine. *Tango* had made it personal. Phil intended to reciprocate.

He looked left and right as his marines cleared the usual bubble, a little larger today because Harinder, Aliza, Kaur, and Heather were all going to make this entrance with him.

He hadn't known setting out, that the gender balance in the *Consensus* was going to be so equal. There were places like

Fribourg where men held all the important roles, and other places where the reverse was true.

Aquitaine and the *Aditi Consensus* were more alike in that than most of the others here. That also helped. Probably frosted the *Gloran Empire* to no end, since they were cut more in the old model of Karl IV's *Fribourg* Empire. Even today those folks referred to that man as *Karl the Mean* in places, where it wasn't simple *Karl the Vicious Asshole.*

Phil stepped forward as the women fell into two wings, like cavalry summoned by trumpets. He smiled at that image and got back a variety of uncertain smiles from folks as he walked into the main auditorium.

Annen Patte had wanted another formal receiving line, like six weeks ago, but Phil had declined. Today was an extended cocktail party, running for about four hours before the kitchen would bring out a buffet and folks would begin to migrate to tables to eat. Markus had escorted Rei Bottenberg down yesterday and put them in charge of the cooking for this event, along with enough marines and sailors to handle everything and ensure that the food was safe.

Assigned Female At Birth, Centurion Rei Bottenberg didn't answer to gender, preferring the non-binary *they* as a pronoun. And they had no higher calling than to cook. To show people around them love by serving them good food.

If tonight's dinner was going to be a little bland by spice load and exotic by culture, everyone would taste Bottenberg's love before they were done.

Heads still turned and conversations fell to nothing. Then the applause started.

Phil stopped walking so he could turn and gesture to Heather. After all, she'd saved lives. He was just in charge and had the brains to hire the right people.

Her blush wasn't quite a supernova, but it was close. Phil was pretty sure she'd get even with him for it when he wasn't looking and it would be fine.

It felt right.

Captain Makara Omarov emerged from the crowd to walk close and bow in the way of the *Dalou* Court. That seemed to break up the crowd and folks went back to what they had been doing, perhaps paying more attention, but still murmuring among themselves.

"Good afternoon, Captain," Phil said.

Heather remained close, while the others began to drift away as folks saw friends or got flagged down. Markus appeared from the mob and slid in close, but stayed largely invisible.

Omarov turned to Heather and bowed again.

"Most impressive work, Command Centurion," he said.

"Thank you," Heather managed.

She was still recovering from everything, which was fine. This conference was his event, once everyone got their chance to speak to *Ground Control*.

"So what is next, First Centurion?" Omarov asked now. "After you complete the social conquest of *Vilahana*."

"Social conquest, Captain?"

"You two are heroes," Omarov said, gesturing at the crowd. "*Ingham* might wish to spread ugly rumors to the contrary, but they were obviously not expecting to be caught at their games. I wondered how soon you might decide to break them."

"Does it matter?" Phil asked the man, feeling something subtle under the *bonhomie*.

"Many privateers and such folks have been known to set up illegal bases in systems claimed by the *Dalou Hegemony*, First Centurion," Omarov replied. "I would expect *Aquitaine* vessels might begin poking around in such regions, at least when you get serious."

"I see," Phil said neutrally. "Would the Shogun be terribly offended if sunlight began to be shone in that direction?"

Not the Emperor. That person was a figurehead from a paternal line dating back to the founding of the Hegemony, but was largely toothless now in terms of power. Everything resided with the Supreme Duke who theoretically commanded all *Dalou* ships, including small-time Knights like Captain Makara Omarov of the Heavy Escort *Morninghawk*.

"It might be a touchy subject, if not approached with great care," Omarov replied in a polite, if evasive tone.

"I understand, Captain," Phil said.

Message received. *Dalou* would appreciate time to perhaps disentangle themselves from some of the things they might have done in the past. Phil considered his next words carefully.

"From here, it is most likely that I will head inward to be received at *Aditi* by the heads of the *Consensus*, Captain," he explained. "Perhaps you will have a chance to report home to both *Serelye* as well as *Ellariel* and explore the possibility of joining us there? This conference will merely introduce all the players and begin to lay the groundwork for future communications and trade. Ambassadors will be delivered and eventually exchanged, with some of them being given letters of introduction to the Senate on *Ladaux*. Remember, nobody knew what to expect when we traveled this far."

"But you intend to remain and continue your explorations?" Omarov pressed. "Set up trade stations here and elsewhere, but travel onward before you return home?"

"Oh, indeed, Captain Omarov," Phil nodded, gesturing to the crowd around them and the approaching Governor Patte and his mob of people. "*Vilahana* was merely the beginning."

READ MORE

Be sure to read the next books in the First Centurion Phil Kosnett series!

Encounter at Vilahana
Consensus at Aditi
Hegemony at Dalou

Available at your favorite retailers!

ABOUT THE AUTHOR

Blaze Ward writes science fiction in the Alexandria Station universe (Jessica Keller, The Science Officer, The Story Road, etc.) as well as several other science fiction universes, such as Star Dragon, the Dominion, and more. He also writes odd bits of high fantasy with swords and orcs. In addition, he is the Editor and Publisher of *Boundary Shock Quarterly Magazine*. You can find out more at his website www.blazeward.com, as well as Facebook, Goodreads, and other places.

Blaze's works are available as ebooks, paper, and audio, and can be found at a variety of online vendors. His newsletter comes out regularly, and you can also follow his blog on his website. He really enjoys interacting with fans, and looks forward to any and all questions—even ones about his books!

Never miss a release!
If you'd like to be notified of new releases, sign up for my newsletter.

http://www.blazeward.com/newsletter/

Buy More!
Did you know that you can buy directly from my website?

https://www.blazeward.com/shop/

Connect with Blaze!

Web: www.blazeward.com
Boundary Shock Quarterly (BSQ):
https://www.boundaryshockquarterly.com/

ABOUT KNOTTED ROAD PRESS

Knotted Road Press fiction specializes in dynamic writing set in mysterious, exotic locations.

Knotted Road Press non–fiction publishes autobiographies, business books, cookbooks, and how–to books with unique voices.

Knotted Road Press creates DRM–free ebooks as well as high–quality print books for readers around the world.

With authors in a variety of genres including literary, poetry, mystery, fantasy, and science fiction, Knotted Road Press has something for everyone.

Knotted Road Press
www.KnottedRoadPress.com

www.ingramcontent.com/pod-product-compliance
Lightning Source LLC
Chambersburg PA
CBHW060248100726
47907CB00003B/807